RUSSIAN SNOWS: COMING OF AGE IN NAPOLEON'S ARMY

Scott Armstrong

DEDICATION
To a camp chest in Savannah
that made all good things possible

Acknowledgements

There are many people who have helped me bring Henri's story to life. I would like recognize them here. Craig Smith who did the cover art; Cindy Trainor and Paul Edward Trainor who were early readers of the manuscript (Cindy also served as the inspiration for Beatrice); Jay Preston who read the story while it was still being written and gave encouragement and advice; my son, Nathaniel, who listened to me read the novel as a bedtime story; my parents, Jack and Donna Armstrong for numerous suggestions and much encouragement. The members of my writers group: Francesca Miller, Jenny Milchman and Kari Miller for crucial guidance, and to the following two group members in particular: Steve Linstrom who read the near-final version and offered helpful insight; and Lizzie Ross who read, analyzed and commented on the near-final version with precision and insight. Also Jean McNamara for general encouragement.

I wish to single out Helen Armstrong, my daughter and Number One NaNoWriMo Writing Buddy. She inspired me to begin this story during National Novel Writing Month in 2010. Her devotion to writing is contagious.

And finally. Sandie Armstrong, my amazing and talented wife without whom this book would not be possible.

Author's Note

This is an account of a fictional French boy named Henri Carle. It is written from his point of view as he tells his grandchildren about experiences that began in 1811 when he was 13 years old. Henri's story includes actual events and incidents that took place during Napoleon's disastrous invasion of Russia. Although Henri was only aware of the things he could see for himself or that someone told him about as the events were unfolding, he has learned more about certain aspects of the campaign over time, which he includes in his story.

While the overall historic events actually happened and some of the characters really lived, the descriptions of them in this book are fictionalized.

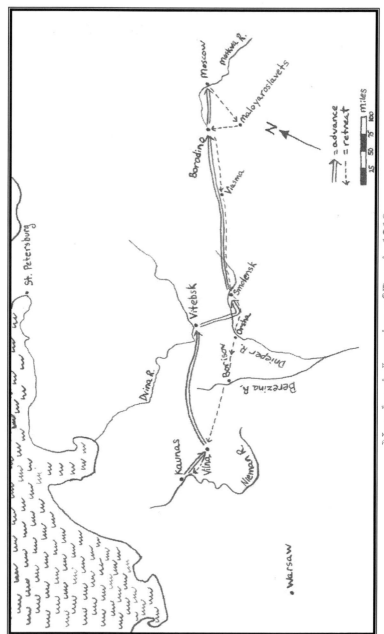

Napoleon's Invasion of Russia 1812

Table of Contents

Prologue - Obernai, Alsace, France, 1868

The winter wind was blowing snow against the side of the house with an angry howl. I turned from the bookshelf and shuffled back to my chair by the fireplace holding a battered but much cherished book. I liked the winters here at the foot of the mountains. The cold gave me an excuse to sit by the fire with my wife and read or reminisce about our long life together. As often happened, the blustery night drew me to the old book I had purchased more than fifty years ago - a book from which all but the first twenty pages were now missing. It reminded me of the blessings of this warm house and my life, especially tonight when our grandchildren were visiting.

When my youngest grandson, Nathanael, saw what I had in my hand, he was disappointed and asked, "Can't you read us an adventure story?"

"Yes, Grandpa, that old book doesn't even have all its pages," my elder grandson, Jaye, pointed out. "Why do you keep it?"

"This book saved my life," I told the boys. "It is part of an adventure that means more to me than any work of fiction."

Jaye looked at me quizzically, but I changed the subject by turning to my granddaughter, Helene, and asking, "What are you studying in school?"

"We are learning about Napoleon Bonaparte and all his victories. He was a great leader from a long time ago," she said.

"Oh, it wasn't all that long ago," I said and then added, "I met him once, you know."

"What!" Helene exclaimed dropping her needlepoint and sitting up straight. "Where?"

"In Russia," I answered calmly.

"Russia?" exclaimed Jaye. "That's thousands of miles from here."

"Was it just you and Napoleon in Russia?" Nathanael asked wide-eyed.

"No. I went there with the Grande Armée of more than half a million men," I answered. "Only 20,000 of us returned," I added staring at the fire and fingering my book.

"What happened to the ones who didn't make it back?" Helene wanted to know.

"Tell us how the book saved your life," my grandsons pleaded.

"It is actually the same story, but it may take a while to tell," I looked at my wife inquiringly.

"There is time before bed if you make it the short version," she said smiling as she put her hand on my arm.

"Yes, my gentle lamb, the short version," I smiled back placing my hand over hers.

"Let's see, it all started in 1811 when I was 13 years old - about your age," I said, looking at Helene. "We lived right here in Obernai. My mother had died that spring so my Aunt Agnes came to live with my father, my brother Luc, and me. Aunt Agnes didn't have children of her own. She seemed cold and distant most of the time. I missed my mother every day.

"Our country had been at war off and on for years, and life was hard. My father had been wounded while serving in the French army. I imagined that he had been wounded doing something heroic, but my father didn't talk about it. Eventually, the injury's lingering effect had forced him to give up farming. He made a meager living working odd jobs. Losing my mother's income as a seamstress was a real blow to the family."

As I continued to talk, I was taken back to that fateful morning. I could see the little room so clearly in my mind, though it was now decades past. When I awoke on that long ago day, I did not know that I would become part of something so vast and tragic that it changed the course of world history.

Chapter 1 - The World Turns Upside Down

The sun was just beginning to show signs of rising on that summer day when I stretched and got out of bed. My older brother Luc was still asleep. He was four years older than me and liked to sleep as much as possible. I heard the voices of my aunt and father talking downstairs. It wasn't the usual everyday conversation. There was an emotional edge to it, and my father sounded upset. Had something happened?

A loud exchange made me hurry downstairs without changing out of my nightshirt. I saw my aunt sitting at our table, straight and proper as usual and my father standing at the fireplace leaning against the mantel with his head hidden in his arm. The room had become quiet upon my entry, and the clock on the mantel, our most valuable possession, sounded loud in the stillness. I stood at the base of the stairs and looked at them, afraid to speak.

My father straightened, turned to me and said, "Go get your brother."

I raced back up the stairs and shook Luc awake.

"Aunt Agnes and Father are arguing about something. They want to talk with us. Hurry." In no time we were downstairs where my father asked us to take a seat at the table.

"As you know," he began, "things have not been going well for our family. Your aunt and I," he said, glancing at my stoic aunt, "do not think we will be able to provide for all of us when things get worse this winter."

"We'll get by," I broke in, "we always do."

My father looked up, smiled weakly, then reached over and gave my arm a squeeze. "Your aunt and I," he continued, "have decided that it is best if you boys were taken care of." He now

1

began to speak faster as if to get out the unpleasant part as quickly as possible. "There is an army recruiting party coming through town today. Luc is old enough to join now and you, Henri, will go along with him. Even though you aren't old enough to enlist, we'll see if we can get you in somehow. We think that at least in the army you will be fed."

Luc beamed. He had talked about joining the military, wearing a handsome uniform and performing feats of bravery. I was stunned. I liked to play at war with my friends re-enacting the many battles France had won under our emperor Napoleon. But I wasn't ready for this.

My father continued. "If I could think of a way to provide for us all, I would do it. Right now, the army offers the best chance." He hung his head. Now he spoke slowly. "Your aunt has gathered together the things you will need and there is a duffel bag for each of you. Go upstairs and get dressed."

I started to say something, but my father gave me a look that said the conversation was over. I followed Luc upstairs. "Can you believe it? We're joining the army and marching to glory!" he said excitedly as he extended his right arm in the air as if holding a sword. I looked at him, not knowing what to say. I felt like I would cry. My life had taken a sharp turn, and I wanted things to go back to the way things were before Mother died.

Luc saw my anguished look. He put his arm around my shoulder and stood next to me. "I know it's hard," he said holding me tight to his side, "but we'll be together. I'll look out for you. It will be the Carle boys seeing the world." That wasn't what I wanted to hear. His arm slipped from around my shoulder. "Look," he said in a serious voice. "Father and Aunt Agnes wouldn't do this if they thought there was any other way. The French army is the best in the world. To be a soldier is the most honorable thing we can do. We'll be fine, you'll see."

Back downstairs, we found my aunt making eggs for breakfast, something we almost never had. I looked at my father. He looked back at me with tears in his eyes. I burst out crying and ran to him, burying my head in his chest. We stood there for a long moment, then he took me by both shoulders and held me at arm's length. "I believe in my boys," he said. "You'll know what to do. I can't be with you, but that doesn't mean I won't be thinking of you."

Breakfast was eaten in silence. There was so much to say, but where to start? I wasn't very hungry and for the first time in my life, couldn't finish a meal.

My aunt brought out the two duffel bags she had packed with extra socks, a thick knit hat and a pair of warm mittens. There was also a thin blanket and tin drinking cup. My aunt put half a loaf of bread on top of each pile for the journey. The sight of the winter hat and mittens reminded me that I would be gone for a long time. My throat began to tighten, and my eyes burned with the effort of holding back more tears.

My father suddenly spoke up, "I know I haven't talked much about my time in the army. I didn't think what I did mattered much here, but there was one thing I learned." He paused and then continued, "Sometimes, the line between victory and disaster is thin. A break one way or another can undo the best laid plans. But, if you are always prepared and thinking ahead, you'll make it through."

"Here, take these," my father added, and he pressed a few coins into each of our hands.

We all walked out into the cool morning and headed for the town square. A crowd had gathered. We weren't the only ones who would be joining that day. I didn't see anyone as young as me, though. My father greeted some of the men he knew, and they looked at Luc and me with satisfaction. The women, though, looked at us with an expression of sadness.

Chapter 2 - Enlistment

The sound of fifes and drums came echoing down the street between the buildings and out into the town square. The musicians were sharply dressed in white and blue regimental coats with lace around the lapels and down the arms. Each wore a sword with a polished handle. Behind them were six soldiers wearing light blue coats. On their heads, they wore tall fur covered hats. They were big men and the hats made them look like giants.

Leading the contingent was a heavy-set officer riding a large gray horse. He looked like he was a few years older than my father. His face was distinguished by a large mustache. He carried his sword in his right hand with the blade resting against his shoulder. Upon a sharp command from one of the drummers, the procession came to a halt. They made a spectacular sight, and the crowd fell silent captivated by the splendor before them. The officer put his sword away, and the sound of the blade echoed around the square as it slid into the sheath and ended with a metallic click. I forgot for a moment why we were there.

Trailing the soldiers at a distance, so as not to be noticed, was a wagon being driven by a tired looking man. Seated next to him was a thin, serious man with glasses and a grim look on his face, clutching a leather portfolio. Even though he wore a uniform similar to the others, he didn't look like much of a soldier. Behind the wagon stood men and boys with duffel bags, knapsacks and blankets. I guessed they were the recruits from previous towns.

The officer rose in the stirrups to begin his speech. "Fellow citizens!" he boomed. "Before you, is an example of the splendor of the French army led by our emperor, Napoleon!" Here, he paused while the crowd cheered. "You know about the victories of the French army: Toulon, Lodi, Arcola, Rivoli, the Pyramids, Aboukir, Marengo, Ulm, Austerlitz, Friedland, Madrid, and Wagram. Today, you are given the opportunity to become a part of this proud and honored profession - to wear the uniform of the Grande Armée!" There was more cheering. The ones who had come to enlist were smiling and elbowing each other.

The officer continued: "The Emperor needs fine young men to step forward and enlist so that the victories may continue and France can reign over her empire." The crowd cheered again, and he concluded, "I now invite all eligible men to step forward to the table and enlist." He held out his hand toward a desk where the serious looking man was sitting. It had been set up during the officer's speech, but no one had noticed. A soldier was standing at attention on either side of a small bench sitting in front of the desk.

There was a rush to be first in line. The first man sat at the bench and began to answer questions from the serious man who then recorded the answers on a sheet of paper. We made our way to the end of the line as a family. Steadily, we moved closer to the front. Then, it was Luc's turn. My breathing became heavier and my throat was tight.

When finished, Luc stood up and stepped aside for me. The man behind the desk was still writing while I sat down. With his eyes on the paper in front of him, he asked me my name. I tried to speak, but couldn't. The man looked up. "What is this? A boy?" he said as he looked over his glasses at me. "The French army does not need a boy." He emphasized the word "boy."

I cleared my throat and said, "Henri Carle."

The man ignored me and said, "How old are you, fourteen? Come back in three years."

"Thirteen, sir," I answered.

"Who is next?" But I was the last one in line. "Be off!" the man said in a loud, angry voice. "You are trying my patience."

My father now stepped forward and said, "Please sir, I want my boys to stay together. It is important to us."

"I don't care about that," the clerk snapped. "My job is to enlist men, not a boy who should be home with a wet nurse." The nearby crowd, including the new recruits, laughed, and the man smiled, pleased with himself.

The commotion had gotten the attention of the officer on horseback. Riding over, he asked the man behind the desk why there was a delay. The clerk began to gather his papers and replied, "I was just talking to one of the local children and encouraging him to enlist when he grows up." The crowd laughed again.

My father had been looking at the officer intently. Finally, he spoke: "Major Briere, sir. Please. I want my sons to enlist together so they can look out for one another." The officer looked at my father.

"How do you know my name?" he asked. My father didn't answer, but Major Briere continued to look at him with his eyes narrowed as if he were trying to make a connection in his mind. "Jacques Carle?" he asked. My father nodded. "You want your boys to enlist together?" Again, my father nodded, this time with an expression of sorrow on his face. The clerk sat frozen, watching this exchange with his papers half way in the portfolio. Briere turned to him and said, "This boy is too young to enlist, but we will take him along and find a place for him with the army. If he is anything like his father, the army needs as many of him as it can find."

The crowd turned to look at my father who was standing with his hat in his hand looking at the ground. My father nodded and said, "Thank you, sir." I looked back and forth between the two of them. How did they know each other? My father had served in the French army during the American War for Independence. They must have known each other from those days, but that was thirty years ago. Major Briere drew his sword, held the hilt to his nose then swept the blade down in a graceful motion. It was a salute to my father.

Major Briere straightened up and yelled, "Form up! All new enlistees take your place at the end of the column." The drums sounded and the new recruits moved to the end of the line. I gasped and fought back tears as my father and aunt hugged Luc and me. Luc took me by the shoulder and led me away. As the column began to march out of the square, I looked desperately into the crowd, but I could not find my father.

Chapter 3 - Recruiting Party

The column continued out of town heading north past some of the familiar places where Luc and I had played. Once we passed out of our town, we stopped, and the soldiers climbed into the wagon. They weren't going to walk to the next town, but we were.

The soles of my shoes were worn thin, and I could feel the stones in the road. The day began to get hotter. The column stopped every few hours so we could drink from a stream. Nobody had a canteen.

Gradually, the feeling of sadness eased, and I started to get hungry. Luc reached into his duffel and pulled out a piece of bread and some egg wrapped in a cloth. "Aunt Agnes thought you might feel hungry later," he said as he handed me the bundle.

Some of the recruits looked around and nudged each. "How about sharing some of your army rations, General?" one of the boys said mockingly. Luc shot him a look that caused the boy to smirk and turn back to his buddies.

As we approached the next town, the Sergeant, whose name was Bayard, came back along the column and spoke to us. "We are going into this town to find more lucky beggars like yourselves," he said. "Stay back out of the way. Don't talk to anyone, don't wander off. You are enlisted soldiers now despite your sorry appearance. Wandering off will be considered desertion and the penalty for desertion is death." He grinned and turned back to the head of the column.

The scene from Obernai was repeated. We left the town to the sounds of cheers from the crowd and cries from distraught mothers. The days continued on this way as we marched first north, then west. Our column of recruits grew with each stop.

Two or three times a day we would be fed. A basket of bread along with potatoes or radishes would be produced, and everyone would crowd around. Once, when neither Luc nor me got a share, Luc wanted to tell the Sergeant. A group of older boys were standing nearby and one of the bigger ones with reddish hair said mockingly, "Wots da matta? Did sumbody's mommy forget to feed him?" The other boys in his group laughed. The boy was looking straight at me. "Better go tell your mommy."

My face burned with embarrassment. I was afraid of this mean boy who had singled me out for ridicule. I wished I could just sink into the ground and disappear.

"Leave him alone!" Luc growled.

"Oh, are you the big bruver? Why don't you both go hide behind mommy's skirt?" the big boy said.

One of the boys in his group said, "Good one, Gaston."

Luc walked up to Gaston, and they stood chest to chest. Gaston was looking down on Luc. "Do you have a problem?" Gaston said through clenched teeth.

Luc replied through his own clenched teeth, "Leave us alone."

"Is there someone here who can make me?"

Just then, a loud voice said with authority, "I can." Everyone turned to see Sergeant Bayard glaring at us. Luc and Gaston stepped apart. "There will be no fighting. Do you know what the penalty for fighting is?" He paused and looked around at the group before saying, "Death."

"I don't have time to take care of a wandering nursery. The next one who gives me trouble is going to get a thrashing before we shoot him. Now form up into a column and let's go."

The lack of food combined with the intense heat made for a miserable day. I often found myself wondering what my father was doing or what I would be doing if I were with him. I might have been just as hungry, but at least I would have been home.

We halted at dusk that day, outside a large town. The cart went on ahead and returned with a basket of bread. This time Luc and I made sure we received our share and ate the day old bread with vigor. There wasn't any water around. The day of walking and the hard bread soon worked up a powerful thirst in everyone.

The sergeant came back to us and said, "We're staying here for the night. Find yourselves a comfortable tree to sleep under."

One of the recruits said, "We need water."

The sergeant looked over the group and said, "Didn't you bring your canteens? If you're thirsty, that isn't my problem." As he spoke, he lifted his canteen and took a long, satisfying drink, wiped his mouth, and sighed, "That was good." Then he strode off. I wasn't liking army life so far, and I wasn't even in the army.

Luc and I found a large tree a little ways off from the group. We settled down with our backs against the tree and just stared. Off in the distance, we could see the mountains, just like at home.

"Why did father have to send us off like that?" I asked quietly.

"You know he had to. With his health the way it is there wasn't any way he could support us this winter when things will get even harder. At least in the army, we'll have a place to stay and food to eat." After he said this last part, we both looked at each other and broke out laughing. Here we were, sitting under a tree where we would have to spend the night. The only food in our stomachs all day had been the hard bread we'd just eaten, and we didn't have anything to drink. The army wasn't doing such a good job of taking care of us.

When we were done laughing, Luc continued, "You know I'd been talking to father about letting me enlist. I didn't know you would be pulled into it with me. I'm sorry."

"I know he did what was best." I replied. "And I am glad you and I are together."

"That's right, and we will stick together."

I smiled as I leaned back and fell asleep.

Chapter 4 - A Taste of Army Life

When I woke at dawn the next morning, I saw a herd of sheep coming toward us. I nudged Luc awake and said, "Look. I bet the shepherd knows where there is a stream." We stood up and approached him as he crossed the road.

"Excuse me," Luc began in a whisper. "Do you know where we can get some water?"

The shepherd was about ten. He looked at us and then at some of the sleeping figures from our party. "Sure," he whispered back. "About a quarter of a mile from here is a stream. Are you escaped convicts?"

"No." Luc replied in a flat whisper, "We're soldiers in the Emperor's army."

The shepherd looked at us doubtfully. "If you say so," was all he said.

We followed the shepherd and his flock across an open field to a quiet stream. After a good, long drink, we thanked the shepherd and headed back across the field. It was brighter now, and when we got near the road, everyone was up and stretching.

Luc and I headed toward the tree where we'd left our duffels. As we walked past Gaston's gang, he called out, "I see you boys decided to join us again." I looked hard at Gaston and noticed he was wearing my socks tied together around his neck like a scarf and had my winter hat perched on top of his head. "Brrr," he said rubbing his arms and pretending to shiver. "I sure am glad my mommy packed my warmys," he said in the mock child's voice he had used before. "The summer can get pwitty cold." His buddies roared with laughter.

11

"Give them back!" Luc shouted as he lunged at Gaston. Two of Gaston's bigger friends stepped in front of Luc and blocked his way. "I said give them back!"

The commotion had attracted the sergeant's attention. "What's going on here?" he demanded as he arrived on the scene.

"They stole our things!" Luc shouted.

Gaston was no longer wearing my socks and hat. They were lying in the road a few feet from him with some of our other stuff. "Who stole what from you?" Bayard demanded.

"He did," Luc said pointing at Gaston. "And the others too. They took those out of our bags."

Gaston spoke up, "Are these yours?" he said pointing at the items on the ground. "They were just here in the road. I was wondering who dropped them."

Sergeant Bayard looked at Luc and me and said, "Pick them up, and be more careful next time."

As we stooped to get them, Gaston and his friends stifled laughs. I could hear some of them saying, "Yeah, be more careful next time."

Although most of the contents of our duffels were recovered, I couldn't find my tin cup. Gaston had taught us a valuable lesson, though. We didn't let the duffels out of our site again.

The number of new recruits began to grow until there were at least 100 of us. One day, we approached the largest town yet and were met by some soldiers in different uniforms and a whole fife and drum corps. While the recruiting contingent went into town, two soldiers escorted us through the streets. One introduced himself as Sergeant Francois LaGrand. He said he was now in charge of us.

LaGrand was younger than my father, on the short side and looked like a veteran of many years' service. On his left hip was a sword, and he carried a musket with a fixed bayonet. From the way he carried it, I got the feeling that musket never left his hand.

Soon we came into a large, open plaza in front of the most magnificent cathedral I had ever seen. Every inch was carved with a design or statue. Someone said we were in the city of Reims.

LaGrand stopped us in the middle of the plaza and announced, "I want you to form a column, five abreast, that means shoulder to shoulder, and we are going to see how well you can march."

We began to move about to get into line as he had asked. The problem was, some of us did not have a concept of the number "five." Luc and I had gone to school so we could tell when there were five in a row. The same couldn't be said for most of our fellow recruits.

The group continued to jostle and shove. I could hear recruits saying, "Can't you count?" "Five in row, dummy. Does this look like five to you?"

The local citizens passing through the plaza were watching the proceedings with amusement. Sergeant LaGrand, fed up with our bumbling, bellowed, "Attention!" We all froze where we were and stood up straight. "All right you bumpkins," he continued. "I can see you are all officer material. Now, let's do this right. We are going to head off in that direction," he said pointing. "I want you to line up facing that way with five of you bums in each row. Now I bet most of you scoundrels have five fingers on at least one of your hands. I want you to hold up the hand that has the five fingers," he held up his hand with his fingers spread far apart, "and find four other fools and line up facing that way," he pointed again in the direction he wanted us to go, "so that there is one rascal in line for every finger on your hand." He added in a flat, tired monotone, "Don't forget to count yourself."

"Now, fall in!" We all began to scramble about again and eventually got into ranks of five. Judging by the difficulty of this maneuver, however, it seemed some of our group were missing fingers or had extras.

When we were all lined up and facing the same direction, Sergeant LaGrand addressed us again, "When I say 'march,' I want you to all begin walking forward starting with your left foot. Now,

I suspect most, if not all, of you have two left feet so you are wondering which one to start with. Well, you should start with the one closest to me."

"To the front. March!" he shouted.

Upon hearing the word "march," most of the column moved forward and with their actual left foot leading the way. Some, however, were gawking at a group of young maids making their way across the plaza, and they were run into from behind by men who were trying to get a last look at the cathedral. When one recruit stumbled into another in this manner, the rest of the column bunched up until everyone got his feet back under him. The column contracted and expanded over and over as we left the plaza and headed down a side street.

LaGrand tried to keep us away from the crowded streets so there wouldn't be too many witnesses to our sorry military appearance. When we did cross some of the larger streets, people stopped to watch and make comments - none of them very flattering. When we approached these streets, LaGrand would begin to call out "Left... left... left, right, left," as a way to keep us in step, or at least more in step than we otherwise were.

I happened to be on the end of one row, next to Luc. Since I was the smallest, I attracted a fair amount of attention - often from women who I imagined had children of their own.

At one of these streets, I noticed that a group of girls about my age had caught sight of me and began talking with their heads together. I straightened up a bit and paid extra attention to the cadence LaGrand was calling out. All of a sudden, I felt someone step on the back of my shoe. My heel slid out, and I stumbled as I tried to keep my shoe from falling off. The shoe stayed on, but the heel of my foot was sticking out, and my shoe threatened to come off with each step. I bent down and tried to work the back of my shoe into place. Since I had to keep marching, I ended up hopping and skipping while doubled over. By the time I got my heel where it belonged and straightened up, I saw that the girls were now laughing and pointing at me. I boiled with rage.

14

Chapter 5 - Getting Even

I was sure the person behind me had stepped on my shoe on purpose. When we halted, I slowly turned my head. I wasn't surprised to see it was one of Gaston's gang. "Where did you learn to march?" he said while grinning down at me. I heard a few laughs from Gaston and his cronies.

My ears were burning from embarrassment and anger, but there wasn't anything I could do. I turned back to the front as LaGrand gave the order to march.

On the far side of the city, ten large wagons waited for us near an improvised table set up on some barrels. We all filed past and received bread, cheese and a piece of ham. Luc filled his tin cup at a water pump nearby, and we sat down in the shade to enjoy one of the best meals we had had in long time. At last, we were eating better than at home.

We talked about the trouble we had been having with the "Gaston gang" as we decided to call them. "Don't worry," Luc said, "we'll get them back."

Soon, LaGrand was calling us to fall in. He explained we would be riding in the wagons to a training camp just outside of Paris. The day was very hot, and even though the wagon jolted us at every bump, we were glad to be riding.

As evening approached, the wagons pulled over near a group of large sheds where we would stay for the night. Luc and I took note of which shed the Gaston gang was in and made sure we got one far away from it.

The night was hot, and we kept the windows open to let in a breeze. When everyone was asleep, I nudged Luc and whispered, "You know those chickens we saw poking around earlier?"

"So?" he said a little too loud.

"How about we take them for a little visit with the Gaston gang?" I made a motion with my head toward the open window.

Luc grinned and nodded. Outside, we each grabbed an unsuspecting chicken and hurried to Gaston's shed. The back window was open as ours had been. Looking at each other, we mouthed the words, "One, two, three." On "three," we both heaved our chickens through the open window.

The chickens began a frantic attempt to escape. The inhabitants were startled awake by beating wings and sharp claws as the chickens went back and forth becoming more and more desperate. The recruits swung their arms and legs for protection, which drove the chickens into more of a frenzy.

Luc and I raced back toward our shed. As we rounded the front corner, there, leaning next to the door and preparing his pipe was Sergeant LaGrand. Luc and I froze. LaGrand lit his pipe, looked up at the clear night sky, and remarked, "Quite a commotion over there."

We nodded. LaGrand continued, "We'll be arriving at camp tomorrow. Don't you think you boys best be getting some sleep?"

We bid him a hasty goodnight and ducked inside. Moments later, running footsteps could be heard coming around the back of our shed and stopping in the front. Through the door, we heard LaGrand say, "Good evening gentlemen. Sure is a warm night to be out running around. Is there something I can do for you?"

We could hear a few mumbled "no's" and then LaGrand continued, "We have a big day tomorrow. Try to get some sleep."

Luc and I looked at each other and then sank down in our places. That LaGrand sure saw more than he let on.

The next day, we passed more and more houses and villages. Late in the afternoon, we were stopped by some soldiers manning a small building by the side of the road. They spoke with the lead driver, and we were waved through. As we passed, the soldiers shook their heads. I wondered what they meant by that.

We continued down a tree-lined road to a large field. Ahead of us was a huge army camp. We passed through a gate in the high wooden wall that surrounded the camp and stretched our necks to get a better view. As far as we could see there were tents, parade grounds, buildings with flags flying in front of them, buildings with smoke coming out of the chimneys, formations of men marching every which way. A squadron of hussars rode past us. Somewhere, we could hear the boom of cannons. Closer by I could hear the metallic clanking of a blacksmith.

None of us said a word.

The wagons stopped at an open area that had a house at one end. Well dressed officers were moving briskly in and out of the house. Some off-duty soldiers had gathered to watch the wagons arrive. We were ordered to dismount and form two ranks. LaGrand walked up and down our lines and attempted to straighten them up. When he was finished, he stepped back to the front and addressed us.

"My original plan was to leave your pathetic carcasses out by the sentry post and sneak away like I'd never seen you before in my life. But they saw me, so here I am with you for a few more minutes." I was getting the feeling that, deep down, Sergeant LaGrand was beginning to like us.

He looked at our ranks one more time, then turned toward the porch of the house and nodded.

Chapter 6 - Camp Arcola

A handsome and well dressed officer walked to the front of our group and stood looking up and down the rows. He began to speak in a voice that said he was better than us.

"I see the gutters of France are now empty," he began, "I am Major Pagnol. You are at Camp Arcola. Here you will be turned into soldiers of the Grande Armée. The Grande Armée has a long and proud tradition. Its success relies on turning miserable wretches into the finest soldiers in the world. Should you fail to reach our standards, you will be dispatched to the Navy where you will serve alongside the ships' rats. I pray you will be more useful to the empire than the rats."

With that hearty welcome still ringing in our ears, he continued, "You will be assigned to training units where the monumental task of turning you into soldiers will take place. Are there any questions?"

One recruit raised his hand and began to say, "Well sir, I was wunderin'...," and his voice trailed off as Pagnol fixed him with the iciest stare I had ever seen. The recruit dropped his hand and looked at the ground.

"Good. I didn't think there would be any questions." Turning to a young officer nearby, he said, "Lieutenant, take charge of the men." As Pagnol started to walk back to the house, he noticed me standing in the back rank. He stopped and said, "You there. Come here."

I went to stand before him. I could feel all eyes on me. "What are you doing here?" Pagnol asked in a cool tone.

"I joined the army with my brother. My father..." But Pagnol cut me off.

"Is a fool," he finished the sentence for me. "Lieutenant, please find a place to keep this child safe until morning then send him back where he belongs." With that, he turned and headed to the house.

I could hear Gaston and his gang stifle laughter, but the lieutenant shot them a look, and the laughter came to an abrupt halt. This wasn't a place to mess around.

The lieutenant turned to me, and I was sniffing back tears. In a quiet voice he said, "Keep your chin up. They never should have brought you here. Just wait while I get the rest of the men sorted out, and then we'll find a way to get you home."

Although I missed my father and home, I wanted to remain with Luc. I watched anxiously while the recruits were formed into small groups. I saw Luc step forward when his name was called. He looked back at me as his group marched off giving me a look of concern, then a nod of encouragement.

When the Lieutenant finally turned back to me, I was determined. "Sir?" I began with my voice cracking just a little. "I want to stay with my brother. My father wanted us to join together. I am a good worker, and I learn fast. Isn't there something I can do here?"

He looked at me for a long time. "My name is Lieutenant Faber. You've made it this far. I think I know a way for you to stay."

Faber glanced toward the house that was the camp headquarters and then led me in the opposite direction. As we walked, he told me about the camp. It was named for one of Napoleon's first victories after being appointed commander of the French Army of Italy. The camp was used as a staging ground to re-organize existing units of the army as well as train new recruits. There were about 30,000 men at the camp along with horses and support staff. This made it larger than most French towns. The camp supported itself with its own blacksmith shop, armory, farm, wheelwright, butcher shop, carpentry shop, cobbler and bakery.

It was to the bakery that we were heading. Lieutenant Faber told me that the man who ran it, Leo Gerrard, was always in need of help. Baking for so many men was a very long process, and Faber didn't think my age would matter as long as I could do the work.

We approached a door in a low, brick building. Faber leaned in and yelled, "Gerrard!"

A large man of about forty came to the door wiping his hands with the bottom of the big white apron he was wearing. "Ah, Pierre, what can I do for you?"

"I have a young man here, Henri Carle, who needs a job and a place to stay. Can you help?"

Gerrard looked at me. "Hmm. I think we can find something. Come," he said motioning for me to step inside. Turning back to Faber, he said, "Don't worry, I'll look out for him."

Lieutenant Faber thanked him, wished me luck, and headed off.

I turned to look at Gerrard. "Call me Leo," he said. "Have you ever worked in a bakery before?"

"No," I answered, "but I've seen my mother bake bread at home."

"Ahhh. That's good enough. Now imagine your mother baking bread for thousands of troops. Here we have five ovens. We'll fire them up tomorrow morning and while they're warming, we'll prepare the dough in there." He pointed to a larger room. "You'll learn as we go along," he continued. "Now, where is Ned?" he asked one of the nearby men.

"Out fetching more flour," was the reply.

"When Ned gets back, I'll introduce you. He's my son and he's about your age. He can show you the ropes."

After a few minutes, two men and a boy walked in. Each had a sack over one shoulder that they proceeded to drop on a table. The boy was a little bigger than me. He had light hair and an energetic look on his face. Leo looked up from what he was doing and said, "Ahhh. Ned, there is someone I want you to meet.

"Ned, this is Henri. Henri is going to be working here and living with us. You need to show him what to do and where to sleep."

Ned smiled at me and said, "Nice to have someone my own age around. You and I are going to have some fun," then, glancing at his father, added, "after our work is done."

Ned showed me around and explained that our jobs would be to get the oven fires going each morning, a task that would start several hours before dawn. Once the first loaves were ready, we would help to deliver the bread throughout the camp.

"Where do you live?" I asked.

"We have a house out back, but most nights I sleep in the wood pile until it gets too cold. Leo doesn't mind because that way I can keep an eye on the wood so it doesn't get stolen."

"Who would steal wood?"

"How long have you been with the army?" he asked raising his eyebrows.

"I've lost track. A few weeks, I guess," I answered, realizing I didn't even know what day it was.

"Well, in the army if it ain't nailed down, it's gonna get stolen and sometimes, when it is nailed down they'll steal it anyway along with the nail."

"But don't they have their own wood?" I asked.

"There's never enough to go around, especially nice, split wood like ours. The men want the wood for their campfires, the butcher wants it to smoke the meat, the kitchens need it to cook."

As I pondered this, I began to feel even more alone. Leo and Ned seemed nice, but I barely knew them. I didn't know where Luc was, and my father was hundreds of miles away. Ned must have sensed I was having mixed feelings about being there. He gave me an encouraging pat on the shoulder and showed me the pile of straw in the wood stacks where we would bed down.

After that Ned taught me how to lay the fires for morning, and then it was time for supper. Behind the bakery was the small house where Leo's family lived. The house belonged to the army, but as the head of the bakery, Leo was able to live there close to where he worked. Ned introduced me to his mother, Nannette, and his older sister, Cressida. Cressida was about sixteen, and she glanced at me before turning back to her sewing.

Supper was a thick soup, bread and cider. Everyone joined in the talk and laughter. It felt good to be at a family table, but soon Madam Gerrard was telling Ned it was time to go to sleep. The ovens wouldn't light themselves.

Chapter 7 - Exploring

Someone was shaking me awake. With all of the effort I could muster, I opened my eyes and began to work out where I was. It was still dark. Very dark. I didn't even hear any roosters crowing. Why was Ned waking me up?

"C'mon. Time to get to work."

Oh yeah, the bakery. But why so early?

My eyes shut again, but Ned was persistent. He had put on his shoes and was poking me with his foot. "It's time to get the fires going," he explained.

I did remember that we had prepared the wood in the ovens so they could be lit in the morning, I just didn't know it would be the part of the morning I called the middle of the night.

"How do you know it's time?" I asked hoping for a delay.

"I just know. Now get up."

"Wait. I'm coming." I said as I pulled on my shoes.

We lit the oven fires and soon the rest of the workers arrived. Before long the smell of baking bread set my stomach to growling. Ned noticed. "Don't worry," he winked, "one of the best parts of this job is getting a whole baguette to ourselves while we make our deliveries."

When the bread was ready, we loaded it onto carts and started our rounds of the many different kitchens around the camp. As the sun rose, the activity level in the camp increased. Ned greeted everyone, the laundry ladies as well as the officers, and almost everyone knew him by name. By late morning, we had delivered our last cartload. It felt like we had pushed the carts ten miles, and I was ready to crawl back into the woodpile and sleep for the rest of the day.

Ned had different plans. "We can't sleep now," he said. "The best part of the day is here."

With Ned as my guide and no carts to push, we started off to explore the camp. First we went to the grand parade ground where we saw new recruits drilling. I looked for Luc among the ranks but didn't see him. Ned assured me that the training schedule for recruits included many different things, and we would be sure to see him there sometime.

As we continued through the camp, Ned explained everything we saw. We watched the cavalry practice a strange drill in which they tried to knock sacks from the top of posts with their sabers. We also saw cannon crews practice firing at targets. As we walked, I kept looking for Luc.

Ned saw me searching and the expression on my face. "Don't worry," he said, "we'll find him. It's a big camp, but we're bound to run across him. C'mon, we better get back for some supper."

The routine continued for about a week: getting up in the pre-dawn hours to light the ovens, delivering the bread, and then spending the afternoon exploring the camp. Ned told me Napoleon had started his military career in the artillery and still favored it. According to Ned, French artillery was the best in the world.

We came so often to watch the cannon crews that some of them would wave to us when we arrived. One day, a gun crew was missing some men and was unable to keep up with the other crews.

The sergeant in charge motioned to Ned and me. We jumped up and hurried over. "Would you two be willing to give us a hand today?" he asked. "A few members of our crew have reported for sick call."

We wanted to shout "YES!" but were afraid to appear too eager. Instead Ned replied, "I guess we can help out."

The sergeant gave us our assignments, and we practiced going through the loading motions a few times without using ammunition, something he called a "dry run."

Then it was time for the real thing. I had watched the process so many times over the past week that I knew exactly what everyone was to do. Doing it, however, was harder than I thought. I found myself running up with the powder too soon or too late, and once, I ran into one of the other gunners. When I got used to the rhythm, though, I darted back and forth right on time. The crew complimented me on my quickness.

Ned did well with his part too, and before long the gun was able to keep up with the others on the firing line. Time flew by and soon it was late afternoon.

Ned and I hurried back toward his house. We were covered with black powder, and our ears were ringing, but we had never been happier. As usual, we stopped at the grand parade ground to look for Luc. Every other time we had been there, I had left with a heavy heart filled with disappointment and frustration. Where could he be? What if something terrible had happened to him?

As these thoughts swirled through my head, I saw him! I jumped up and down waving my hat in the air shouting, "Luc!" Luc's head didn't move, but I could see a look of surprise come over his face. The drill sergeant looked in my direction with a scowl.

Ned said, "Let's wait and follow them back to their camp."

After what seemed like hours, the sergeant looked up at the setting sun and marched his men off the field. We followed them through the camp to a row of tents. As soon as the men were dismissed, Luc ran over and hugged me.

"What are you doing here?" Luc exclaimed. "I thought they sent you home."

I told him about my job at the bakery and introduced Luc to Ned. Luc looked at the black powder stains on my hands and clothes. "What else do they have you doing?" he asked.

I told him about our experience with the gun crew. He shook his head and said, "They haven't even let me hold a gun yet. All we do is march and then march some more. They wouldn't even let us use the grand parade ground until today."

Luc looked good in his uniform. He wore a blue and gold coat, white shirt, vest, and pants that fastened over his shoes. The uniform was well worn, and we joked that it looked old enough to have been in America with our father. I asked if his initials were sewn into it. "No, I checked," Luc laughed.

"I'm writing to Father," he said. "I haven't sent the letter yet. I work on it a little each evening. I'll tell him you are here and safe." Upon saying the word "safe," he looked at my powder stains and added with a grin, "Well, I'll tell him you're here anyway."

"Tell father I miss him and think about him every day. He shouldn't worry. I'm staying with a good family."

That night, for the first time in weeks, I fell asleep content.

Chapter 8 - Making the Rounds

I continued to see Luc a few times a week in the evenings. Ned and I visited the artillery firing range every chance we got. We were able to fill in a few more days with "our" gun crew until the regular members returned from the hospital. The other crews had seen us at work so they invited us to join their crews when they were short a man or two. We got to try different positions around the gun and soon had experience with everything. Sometimes they even let us aim.

Watching the hussars was one of our favorite things. They often practiced the bag-on-post drill with sabers or lances. I had figured out that the bags represented enemy soldiers' heads, and I was glad I would not have to face them in battle. On other days, they would practice riding in formation and firing from horseback with a pistol and a short musket called a carbine.

We liked to follow them back to the stable and help care for the horses. The soldiers would flip us a few coins for doing this, and they would tell us stories of their commander, the dashing and flamboyant King of Naples, Joaquin Murat, a marshal of France. He wore bright, fancy uniforms and, according to them, performed feats of bravery on a daily basis. They spoke of him with awe, and I didn't doubt his men would have followed him anywhere.

They also talked about how he turned the lady's heads in every town they passed. They didn't go into many details on that last part, but I noticed they would all smile and chuckle to themselves.

One day, after the hussars had been practicing sword fighting on horseback, I overheard one of the officers, Captain Vallon, complaining about some braid that had been torn loose from his coat. I approached him later and said in a small voice, "I can fix the braid for you."

"You can?" he said sizing me up.

"My mother was a seamstress, and I used to help her. Let me take your coat, and I'll have it back here tomorrow morning."

Still eyeing me, he took off the coat and handed it to me. It was heavy! I almost dropped it when he put it in my outstretched hand.

"I'm more worried about your ability to carry the coat home than your sewing ability," he joked. "Just drape it over your shoulders like a cape, and it will be easier for you to carry," he suggested.

I did as he said. With the coat on my shoulders, I felt transformed. I was no longer a boy working in a bakery. I was an officer of the hussars. My mind began to run wild with imagination: I was leading a charge into the teeth of the enemy lines, then I was on parade at the head of the hussars while the crowds cheered and threw flowers. Just as Marshal Murat and I were reviewing our troops, I was snapped out of my daydream by Ned saying it was time to go to supper.

As we walked through the camp, the sight of a boy wearing the braided uniform of a hussar officer drew quite a bit of attention. There were some good-natured calls of greeting, and some that were downright mean. I ignored the mean ones and walked a little taller for the good ones.

As we came through the door of the Gerrard house, Ned said, "Guess who got a promotion today?" and everyone turned to look at me as I stood in the doorway, feet apart, hands on hips, with my chin lifted and head turned dashingly to the side. My grin grew and grew until it turned into uncontrollable laughter, and I doubled over as everyone joined in.

After supper, Madam Gerrard gave me needle and thread to sew the braid back in place. When it was done, it looked as good as new. Then, I noticed a tear near the elbow and sewed that up, too.

The next morning, I tucked the coat into the cart when it was time to make the delivery near the stables. I found Captain Vallon talking to some other officers. When he saw me holding the coat, he said, "Ah," with a look of anticipation on his face. "Let's see what you've done."

He took the coat and held it up at arm's length. He smiled as he looked at the braid. Then, examining the elbow of the sleeve where I had made the repair, he looked at me out of the corner of his eye. He pulled out a coin and flipped it to me. "Well done. If you have time, I might have more work for you." I thanked him as I hurried off.

Since I was travelling between the kitchens and officers' messes each morning, I offered to take messages, reports, lists, inventories and small items back and forth as I made my rounds. I saw Lieutenant Faber from time to time. He was always glad to see me and asked how I was getting along and if Luc was doing all right.

Because we moved so widely throughout the camp, Ned and I were tuned in to all of the latest rumors and gossip. Half of the rumors pointed toward an upcoming invasion across the channel to England while the other half were about pending war with Russia. We made sure to pass along all rumors as facts and as a result were well received wherever we went.

Captain Vallon sent more mending business my way, and I soon had to share the work with Madam Gerrard and Cressida. Officers were responsible for purchasing and maintaining their own uniforms and something always needed repair. Sometimes I was up so late working on the sewing that I got only an hour or two of sleep before I had to be at the bakery.

A few times, the Gerrards had Luc over for supper, and I noticed that he and Cressida often stole looks at each other. Our suppers were always happy and filled with lively conversation. Things were going along well, and though I still missed home, I was happy with my situation.

Chapter 9 - The Past Returns

That fall it often rained for days without stopping. The streets of the camp turned into giant mud puddles, and my feet were always wet. The thin wheels of the bread cart sunk easily into the mud making it harder to push.

One morning as the sky was just starting to turn from pitch black to dark gray, I was pushing my loaded cart alone through the rain. As I passed next to the blacksmith shop, I heard a familiar voice saying, "Are you delivering that nice yummy bread to your mommy?" It was Gaston.

I heard footsteps in the puddles behind me. I hoped that if I ignored him, he would go away. But the footsteps were gaining on me and there was more than one pair of feet. I felt a big, cold hand on my shoulder. "What's da matta?" Gaston asked in the mock child's voice he had ridiculed me with before. "Don't you remember your old friend Gaston?"

By now, the others were in front of the cart, blocking my way. "Leave me alone, Gaston!" I said as I tried to squirm out of his grip.

They all reached under the oilcloth and pulled out two baguettes each.

"Put them back!" I protested. "They aren't for you, I have to deliver them."

"Oh, I don't think that's going to happen."

As he said this, Gaston grabbed the handle of the cart and pitched it forward, spilling the bread into a large puddle as his friends howled with laughter. They kicked at the pile until it was a muddy mess. I was blinded by anger. I flew at Gaston with my fists flailing. Gaston was much bigger and shoved me to the ground with ease.

There I sat in a puddle feeling humiliated. I looked at the ruined pile of bread and raged at myself for being unable to protect it. Gaston and his friends headed down the road, eating the bread they had taken and congratulating each other on their fine bit of fun.

I heard running feet splashing through the rain toward me and then Ned was helping me to my feet and righting the cart.

"What happened?" he asked.

Through gritted teeth I told him about Gaston and how I knew him.

"Get it out of your head for now," Ned advised. "We still have deliveries to make, and we better hurry or there could be big trouble."

We decided to turn making the deliveries through the pouring rain into a game, and I almost forgot the earlier trouble. It was a challenge to see how fast we could get to each delivery spot, back to the bakery for the next load and then out again for more deliveries. We were laughing as we put the carts away and argued over who had won the race.

As we helped clean up the bakery, afterward, I realized I didn't feel so good. Though I was still in my soaked clothes, I started to feel very hot. Ned noticed that I wasn't talking anymore. Leo came over and felt my forehead like he was checking an oven. "You could bake bread in there," he said referring to my head. "Ned, get him home and into something dry."

Ned took me into the house where Madam Gerrard went to work drying me off, finding me a thick flannel nightshirt and tucking me into a bed in the corner of the main room. With the sound of the rain pounding on the roof, I slipped in and out of sleep.

I don't know how long I had been lying there when I saw Madam Gerrard standing at the open door talking with a soldier. I closed my eyes again, but then Madam Gerrard was shaking me awake and saying, "Henri, Henri. You've got to get up now. These men have come to take you to see Major Pagnol."

Major Pagnol? My groggy mind was trying to figure out who he was and why I had to go see him when all I wanted to do was sleep.

Madam Gerrard continued, "Someone saw what happened this morning with the bread, and Major Pagnol wants to see you."

Oh, now I remembered. Major Pagnol had been the officer who addressed our recruiting party when we first arrived at camp. He was the officer who told Lieutenant Faber to send me back home. If he finds me here... my thought trailed off as a wave of sweat swept over me.

Madam Gerrard helped me into some of Ned's dry clothes and a jacket. She wrapped an oilcloth around my shoulders. Then Leo walked with me as two soldiers escorted us through the rain to the headquarters building. Once inside, we were instructed to sit on a bench in the hallway. I was so tired and ached so much that my head dropped to my chest, and I dozed.

At one point, I awoke and looked up. There, across from me sat Gaston and two other men who I recognized from this morning. I remembered the anger and shame they had caused, but it seemed hazy and far away. I was so tired and aching that my eyes closed again. Through my sleep, I could hear Leo saying, "Please, he's sick. He needs to be home in bed."

Someone answered, "The Major is very busy. He will see you when he has time."

Much later, a loud voice announced, "Brasheer, Lafleur, Toule, and Carle. The Major will see you now."

Chapter 10 - Injustice

We were shown into a room at the end of the hallway and stood in front of a desk where Major Pagnol was sitting. He studied a paper in his hand and then looked up at us. "Who are you?" he demanded of Leo. Without waiting for a reply, he barked, "Get out of here!" and motioned for a soldier who was standing by the door to escort Leo out. Leo protested, but it was no use.

Major Pagnol looked up at the four of us. "There was an incident this morning where a cart full of bread, army property, was destroyed," he paused to look at each of us, then stood up and began to walk back and forth with hands clasped behind his back. "Destroying army property is a serious matter," he said looking at me. I had been standing with my fists clenched at my side in an attempt to keep from shivering. I was having trouble focusing on him in my fevered state.

Major Pagnol fixed his eyes on Gaston. "Why don't you tell me, Private Brasheer, what happened this morning."

Gaston stood up a little straighter and began, "Well, my comrades and I were on a special errand. It was raining real hard, and we were just going about our business so we could get back to our billet and be out of the rain. The next thing we knew, this bread cart rammed into us from behind and tipped over. Of course, we tried to help this boy clean it up," he said pointing at me. This ridiculous speech woke me up a bit, and I glared at Gaston.

Ignoring me, he continued, "As we leaned over to pick up the loaves that hadn't gotten in the mud yet, he just started yelling at us and punched me. We didn't want to see all that bread ruined, but we couldn't help it," Gaston concluded, shrugging his shoulders.

Major Pagnol dryly asked, "And what do you suppose brought on this sudden and vicious attack?"

"Well, sir. Me and him was signed up by the same recruiting party. He never did like me, and I guess he just thought he could get me."

Pagnol looked at Gaston and his friends and said, "Three soldiers of the Emperor's Grande Armée attacked by a boy from the bakery with a bread cart? Let's hope the English don't hear about this, or they'll come across the channel with an army of bakers."

Turning to me, he continued, "I gave very specific instructions that you were to be returned home, but I see you are still here. Tomorrow morning I shall have you turned out of the camp."

My stomach grew tight and my fevered head felt like it was in a vise. Turned out of camp? Luc was here, I had found a place to stay with a good family, and I was working hard to earn my keep. How could I be thrown out now? I gasped a little and looked at the floor.

"As for you three," he said to Gaston and his accomplices, "perhaps the first week in the stockade will give you time to think about your actions and the second week will allow you to think about how silly you are for supposing that I would believe the story you just told."

Desperate, Gaston began to speak, "But it was him I tell you. He just..." Major Pagnol fixed him with a look that made Gaston's voice trail away into nothing.

"A soldier must have honor, something you clearly lack."

Pagnol made a gesture with his head as a signal and soldiers came filing into the room to escort Gaston and the two others out. The three of them glared at me as they were led away.

Another soldier took me by the elbow, and we turned to go. Leo came in looking worried and confused.

Pagnol spoke to him, "How do you know this boy?"

"He works in my bakery. What is happening?" Leo asked.

"This boy is to be turned out of camp in the morning. He has been here against my orders."

"But he's such a good worker. He never complains, always gets his work done, and he gets along with everyone," Leo pleaded.

"He will spend the night in the stockade and will be turned out in the morning as I ordered when he first arrived."

"But, sir. He is very sick, I can take him home with..."

Pagnol interrupted, "Doesn't your family live in the camp bakery house?"

"Yes, sir."

Pagnol didn't say any more, he just looked at Leo, daring him to speak.

Grasping the threat that Pagnol was making, I said, "It will be all right, Leo. I'll be fine," although, I was far from sure.

The soldier guided me out into the rain. At the door to the stockade, Leo said a quick goodbye, and I was led to a small cell with a wooden pallet for a bed and a metal bowl in the corner. The only thing good about the cell is that it wasn't near wherever Gaston and the others were being kept.

I lay down on the pallet and huddled under the oilcloth. Suddenly, I heard a furious banging on the outside door of the stockade and a woman's voice speaking fast and firm. Next, I heard the lock on my cell being opened, then Madam Gerrard was next to me. She helped me into a dry nightshirt and tucked me under a warm blanket. She stroked my hair as I drifted in and out of sleep. I could feel a cool cloth on my hot forehead.

Madame Gerrard was still with me when I awoke in the morning. My head felt clearer and my body didn't ache as much. I remembered the awful series of events that had brought me here. Madam Gerrard had my duffel bag packed with dry clothes, a bundle of bread, meat and cheese and a bottle of cider.

As I got dressed, I could see there were tears in her eyes, and I began to cry, too. The Gerrards had taken me in and shared all they had. I felt like I was leaving my father all over again.

The jailer hurried to the cell door. With frightened, imploring eyes, he spoke to Madam Gerrard, "Please, I beg you to leave now. They're coming to get the prisoner. If they find you here I'll lose my job."

Madam Gerrard stood and straightened her skirt. I also stood, gave her one last hug, and croaked, "Thank you," through my tears. Then she was gone.

Chapter 11 - Becoming a Teamster

As I was being led out of camp, Lieutenant Faber joined me and whispered that he had found a job for me with the civilian teamsters who drove the supply wagons for the army. He told me to go to their camp on the other side of the north wall of Arcola and ask for Jean-Claude Merrien. Although I would still be nearby, Lieutenant Faber advised me to avoid being seen back in Arcola.

I walked out through the gate alone and headed off following Lieutenant Faber's instructions. The teamster camp wasn't hard to miss. There were stables, bunkhouses and what looked like hundreds of wagons.

I approached a group of men playing cards on the porch of one of the bunkhouses. They didn't notice me walk up, so when I spoke, they all jumped. Playing cards was not allowed at Arcola, and from the way the men reacted, I guessed it wasn't allowed here either.

"What are you doing sneaking up like that, boy?" yelled one gruff man as he slapped down his hand of cards on the makeshift table.

"I'm sorry," I stammered, "I was just looking for someone."

"Well, who is it you're looking for?"

"Jean-Claude Merrien. I was told to look for him by Lieutenant Faber."

"An officer told you to look for Merrien? What's he done and why did they send a boy to find him?" he said as the others laughed.

"He has a job for me."

"I knew things were worse than they're telling us," he said slapping his knee. "Now even the children are pitching in to bail out old Bony."

"I just got thrown out of the camp and need a place to stay."

"Oh, yeah. I remember you. You work at the bakery in camp. I saw you when I was there delivering a load."

"Well, I used to work there. Now I need a job. Can you tell me where I can find Monsieur Merrien?"

The men roared with laughter.

"What's so funny?" I asked.

When the laughter had died down, one of them said, "We ain't never heard nobody call Merrien 'Monsieur Merrien' before. Around here we call everybody by their last names."

They were sure having a lot of fun at my expense, and I was getting tired of being mistreated. "Look, can you tell me where to find him or do I need to keep looking on my own?" I had become more forceful during my time at Arcola.

"Sure. Look in that shack right over there," one of the men said pointing across the way to a small building.

I thanked him and headed over. Knocking on the door, I heard a rough, "Come in," from the other side. I entered, and there, at a desk covered in paperwork, sat a large bear of a man with a full, graying beard that hung down to his chest. "Who are you?"

"I'm Henri Carle. Lieutenant Faber sent me."

He grunted. "Oh, right, I did talk to him. I thought you would be older and... bigger."

"Sorry sir. I expect to grow some," I offered as an apology.

"Hmmph," was all he said as he turned back to the desk. Without looking up he said, "There's a bunk over there," tossing his head to one side. "Put your things down, and I'll show you around."

Merrien explained I would help with the feeding of the horses, the care of the harnesses and anything else that was needed. He told me the job of the teamsters was very important. The troops had to be supplied. We would be travelling a good deal on trips to pick up or deliver supplies and build depots for the army to use when it was on the march.

"Napoleon says the army travels on its stomach and that's true. An army can deteriorate fast when the men are hungry. Discipline breaks down when men begin to go off on their own to find food."

I found out later that Merrien had once been a soldier. He had been wounded in the leg years ago so he switched to the teamsters. Over the next few weeks, we made many supply runs, and I always rode with him. He was gruff and didn't come across as friendly, but he always treated me fairly.

I couldn't say the same for the rest of the men. They muttered when I made a mistake and rolled their eyes if I asked a question. I hated being there, but I had nowhere else to go. It seemed so unfair that they didn't even give me a chance, and I sometime cursed them under my breath using some of the new words I had learned in camp. I resolved to prove to these men that I could carry my weight. Whenever I saw an opportunity to do something extra to help out, I took it, whether it was filling in for someone to do their chores or pitching in to lend a hand without being asked. Gradually, I noticed a change for the better in the men's attitude toward me.

Chapter 12 - Camp Life

Merrien noticed the change, too. He pulled me aside one day and said, "I've been watching you. You've shouldered your share of the work and more without complaining, which is more than I can say for most of my men. Here's something for your hard work." He held out a little cloth sack, and when it dropped into my hand, I could hear the clink of coins. Lots of them.

"Now that you're swimming in money," he said, "Let's get you a new set of clothes. It's getting too cold for your ankles to be hanging out like that."

It was true. The pants I had worn when I came to Arcola were much too short, my shirt was getting tighter, and my vest pulled at the buttons. Plentiful food and exercise had made me grow.

The next morning we set off for the local village. We stopped at a small cottage and knocked. A happy and energetic, red headed woman, a little younger than Merrien, opened the door. Her face lit up when she saw him. She put her arms around Merrien and gave him a big kiss.

"Mademoiselle Mahovlich, I'd like you to meet my friend Henri Carle," he said as he introduced us.

She shook my hand and laughed, then gave me a big kiss, too. "Call me Beatrice," she said. She was the most pleasant person I had ever met.

Merrien continued, "Henri needs a new set of clothes."

"I can see," answered Beatrice holding me at arm's length. "We can take care of that."

She motioned us inside and went over to a basket, pulled out a knotted string, and told me to step up onto a nearby stool and stand still. Using the string, she measured me every way possible.

"You two get back to your work. Tomorrow, come for supper and try on your new clothes," she said as she began to rummage around in a large pile of cloth.

I had been away so much with the teamsters that I had not seen Luc or the Gerrards since leaving Camp Arcola some weeks before. I asked Merrien if I could go into Arcola for a little while if I promised to return for my evening chores.

"Don't get caught. Major Pagnol will be all over my..."

"I'll be careful," I chimed in, "I promise."

Arcola had a high wooden wall all around it, but it wasn't very solid in some places. I doubt the army thought the camp would be attacked since we were so close to Paris. I ducked through an opening near the hussars' stable. A few of the men were sitting around and waved for me to come over. Everyone was laughing, patting me on the shoulder and welcoming me back.

"Did you come to get my shirt to mend?" one of them asked.

"I'll pick it up on the way out," I said, then excused myself and headed for the bakery.

It was late in the afternoon on a cold November day as I knocked on the Gerrard's door. Cressida answered, gave a big smile, then frowned, pulled me inside and slammed the door shut.

"What are you doing here?" she asked in an excited whisper.

"I came to visit," I whispered back. "Why are we whispering?"

"They can't know you're here," she said in a more normal voice. "Someone might turn you in to the Major."

Just then, there were footsteps outside and the door burst open. Cressida and I jumped, but there stood Madam Gerrard.

"Henri!" she yelled and gave me a big hug.

"Mother," Cressida scolded, "what if the Major finds out?"

"Oh, don't worry about him," said Madam Gerrard waving her hand at Cressida. "I hope he has better things to do than track down boys who sneak into camp to visit."

She held me by both shoulders and beamed. "Your brother has been by to visit, and he's doing well. Why haven't you come back before now?"

"I've been on supply trips with the wagon train," I answered. "So Luc has been by?" I asked looking at Cressida who blushed and looked about the room for something that needed straightening.

"We'll set another place for supper," Madam Gerrard said.

"I can't stay, I've got to get back soon for chores. Is Ned around?"

"He and his father are off on some errand," she responded. "How about I fix you up with some bread and a few slices of ham?"

With a bundle of goodies under my arm, I headed back toward the hussar's stable. I kept my head down and stayed off the main streets. I picked up the shirt for mending and slipped out of camp.

The next day, Merrien and I returned to Beatrice's house where I tried on my new set of clothes. They were a perfect fit. "I even left a little tucked into the seams and hem so they can be let out as you grow," she pointed out. They were the first clothes that had been made just for me.

Chapter 13 - Christmas

In early December we took a wagon train of supplies north to a depot in Bavaria. Along the way, I told Merrien I had heard a rumor that the recruits would be assigned to regiments soon. If Luc was in a regular unit, he would be going wherever that unit was sent, and I didn't know how I would be able to stay close to him.

Merrien told me not to worry. "As big as the army is, you have a way of bumping into the people you know from time to time so you can renew acquaintances." He said it would all work itself out. I wasn't convinced.

To take my mind off of it, Merrien taught me how to drive the team. After riding beside him on so many trips, I didn't think it would be that hard. I wasn't prepared, however, for the feeling of power I had with the reins in my hands. I was grateful for the faith he had in me.

When we returned from the supply run, I arranged to have someone else cover my chores so I could visit the Gerrards and stay for supper.

We talked long into the night. The Gerrards wanted to hear all about my trip. I told them Bavaria wasn't all that different from France although the houses looked a little strange the further we went. The mountains were similar to the ones near where I grew up. The Gerrards were surprised to hear that there was snow on the mountaintops all year around.

We talked about the latest rumors about problems with Russia. Russia was on our side, at least for now, but Leo pointed out there were many allies that later became enemies. France had fought a war with Russia just five years earlier.

When I was leaving, Madam Gerrard invited me back for Christmas day. She said Luc would be able to come too as the army traditionally had the day off.

I had made quite a bit of money with my sewing business so I wanted to buy some Christmas presents. I asked Merrien for a suggestion for Luc.

"Socks," was his reply. "You can't put a price on a pair of warm, dry socks when out on campaign."

Beatrice helped me find a good, thick pair in town as well as some gifts for the Gerrards. I was happy that I could finally give them something after all they had done for me.

On Christmas morning, though, I awoke feeling more sad than happy. I was worried that Luc's new unit would be sent to another country. Even though I hadn't seen him much, at least he had been nearby so far.

I jumped down from my bunk and noticed something sitting on top of my duffel bag. It was a pocket knife with a ribbon tied around it. I opened the blade, and it balanced as if it were made for my hand. Merrien was not there, but I resolved to bring him some of our Christmas dinner as thanks.

A thin blanket of snow had fallen overnight, the first of the season. I dressed, grabbed my bundle of gifts, and headed out the door to the Gerrards.

The whole family was there. After wishing them a Merry Christmas, I asked Leo and Ned why they weren't still making and delivering bread. They told me that on holidays, the soldiers often sleep through most of the meals as they try to recover from the celebration of the night before.

A fire was roaring in the fireplace, and the room felt warm and inviting. After a big breakfast, Ned and I went out to do some visiting. We stopped in at a few of the kitchens and chatted for a while then went over to the artillery camp to see our friends there. They told us about strong rumors that everyone would be moving soon and there would be a big campaign in the spring, Napoleon's biggest ever, they said.

The snow had continued falling and the temperature was dropping. I was glad I had my mittens from home. On that warm July day when Luc and I left, it was hard to imagine needing them. The knit hat from home did not fit me so well, however. It no longer covered the bottoms of my ears.

When we arrived back at the Gerrard's, Luc was sitting by the fireplace, with Cressida seated on the floor at his feet. He jumped up and came over to give me a hug. "Wow," he said. "My little brother is getting bigger. It sure looks like you could use this," he said, handing me a new knit hat. He smiled at Cressida, who had clearly made it, and I thanked them both.

Luc was wearing a blue dress uniform with white facings on the front and the cuffs. His long grey trousers almost covered a pair of matching grey gaiters underneath. A black stripe ran down the outside of each leg.

After I had finished inspecting and admiring his new uniform, I asked Luc which regiment it was for. "The 18th Regiment of the line in the 11th Infantry Division," he said with pride.

"Do you know when you'll be leaving and where you'll be going?" I asked.

"Within the week, we will be leaving for Italy," he replied enthusiastically.

Luc was proud of his new regiment and uniform and was eager to join the ranks. I could see out of the corner of my eye that Cressida was staring quietly at the floor. I wasn't feeling too happy either.

Soon we were all enjoying a feast of roast goose, beans and warm bread. I could not remember eating so well in one day before. We spent the rest of the evening singing and talking by the fire. It was hard to leave when the time came for Luc and me to go. I walked with Luc to his barracks. He gave me a hug and said, "Don't worry, we'll meet up again. We won't be leaving for a few more days, come and see me. Oh, and thanks for the socks." Then, he turned and went inside.

Chapter 14 - Parade through Paris

The weeks flew by. On February 23rd, I turned 14, and the Gerrards had a special meal in my honor. I wished that Luc could have been there, but Cressida had a letter from him, and she read parts of it aloud to us. He was doing fine and liked the mild weather in Italy.

The teamsters were very busy picking up supplies and building up depots. Some trips took a few days, but once the spring rains started, the trips were much longer and more difficult. The rain turned the roads into mires, and we spent hours each day pulling the wagons out of the mud.

In mid-May we returned from one such trip to find the large open field across from the teamster camp filled with tents. Camp Arcola had turned into a beehive of activity in our absence. Napoleon planned to have a grand parade through Paris before the army set off on campaign. Troops were assembling from all over. I was excited to find that Luc's regiment was among them.

Everyone was talking about the parade. Even though Paris was near Arcola, I hadn't been there and didn't want to miss a chance to see the splendid sight of so many men in their best uniforms marching through the streets. Luc talked to his lieutenant, Jean Hebert, for whom I had done some mending, and he agreed that I could accompany him as his aide in the parade if I could get something to wear that would match the regiment.

Because the whole army would be leaving on campaign after the parade, the teamsters were thrown into a whirlwind of activity. In spite of this, Merrien made sure I was prepared for a long journey and for my special assignment during the parade. Beatrice made me a uniform like those worn by the 18th Regiment, and

Merrien sent me to the shoemaker to get a sturdy new set of shoes. The shoemaker told me the soles were good and thick so as to last longer on the march. I explained to him that I would be riding in a wagon, but he just nodded knowingly and said, "Everyone walks in the end."

I visited the Gerrards one last time to say goodbye. Madam Gerrard prepared a big supper and also wrapped up some bread and meat to take along. She gave me a thick bottle with a cork and made me promise to always keep it full and in my haversack until I could get a canteen.

With tears in our eyes, we said farewell. I was excited about the future, but scared about the unknown. The Gerrards had become as close as family to me, and that made it even harder to leave.

Because of the large number of troops involved, I had to stay with Luc's regiment the night before the parade. After dark, we began marching to Paris. Along the way, we stopped for a few hours of sleep while other regiments marched by to get into position. Soon it was time to form up again. "Quickly, lads!" Hebert shouted, "We'll be stopping again before we enter Paris so don't worry about making yourselves look pretty now."

I heard one of the men giving another a hard time about how a few hours would be needed to make him "pretty" and how he hoped Napoleon wouldn't mind if we were late. I turned to Hebert and asked, "Is Napoleon really going to be there?"

Hebert said, "I'm only a lieutenant so the Emperor doesn't tell me his plans, but I assume he will be there to review this many troops in the capital."

We arrived on the outskirts of the city as the sun rose. The order was given to halt and make final preparations for the parade. Packs were adjusted, cartridge boxes settled and last minute pipe clay applied to the white cross belts that hung over each shoulder. Lieutenant Hebert put on a pair of white leather gloves and adjusted the collar of his uniform.

Up and down the column, the ensigns removed the regimental colors from their cases and unfurled them in the breeze. The musicians were taking the opportunity to re-tighten their drums and were testing them with a few cadences.

Then, from up in front the word "attention" was shouted and picked up by officers as it made its way down the column. Everyone snapped to attention. We could hear the drums begin their cadences as the front of the column began to move. Soon it was our turn. Our colonel give the preparatory command, "To the front," which was echoed by the officers through our whole regiment. Then, the single word "March!" and we stepped out as one with the beat of the drums.

It was late May, and the day was as bright as any I had seen. The sight of regiment after regiment, all in parade dress and with fixed bayonets took my breath away. Crowds cheered and threw flowers to us as we marched up the Champs Elysées. Napoleon was there reviewing the troops. As we passed, I tried to catch a glimpse of him from my place next to Lieutenant Hebert, but we went by too quickly.

We continued to march through the city and the crowds became thinner. We were on the outskirts as night fell.

We slept in an open field without tents. Luc and I talked about how proud our father would be of the two of us. We were part of what had to be the most splendid and powerful army in the world. Lying in the grass next to my brother, I fell asleep happy.

Chapter 15 - Across Europe

T he next morning, I said goodbye to Luc and rejoined Merrien and the wagon train. Three of our wagons had been requisitioned by a general and were filled with furniture, tents, books, food and other goods just for him. It seemed some members of the army would be campaigning in comfort.

Our train moved independently of the army. We would often leave before them in the morning and arrive at our destination first. We almost always slept with the wagons in order to watch over them and the horses. Common soldiers were not given tents on campaign, so they stayed in local houses and barns, if they were lucky. Because it was May, the crops were just starting to grow in some of the fields the soldiers camped in. The farmers pleaded with the officers to keep the men out, but they often had to watch helplessly as the season's planting was trampled.

Villages sometimes welcomed the troops by bringing out wine, bread and cheese to the town square for the men. They hoped this would appease the troops and put them on better behavior while they were billeted in town. In spite of the generosity, chickens and geese were often stolen along with clothing and other household goods. I thought about how my father would get along if his house were plundered, and I felt embarrassed to be part of the army.

We never stayed anywhere more than one night and had soon crossed through the thick forests of western Europe. As we headed east across open plains, the roads turned into little more than goat trails, and the towns became sparse. The people seemed much poorer, but they were happy to see us. Merrien said we were in Poland, and the peasants thought we had come to give them their freedom. "I'm afraid they'll be disappointed," he concluded.

We saw thousands of troops each day, and most were not French. They were from the many states and countries that made up Napoleon's empire. Not many of them spoke French, and we didn't speak their languages. Sometimes, this led to disagreements over lodgings, right-of-way and other matters. The veteran teamsters kept remarking on how they had never seen so many troops all heading in the same direction.

Around mid-June, we stopped in one of the larger towns, and I recognized the flag of the 18th Regiment outside one of the houses. I had not seen Luc since the parade so Merrien gave me permission to go search for him.

When I found him, the first thing I noticed was how tired he looked. I shouldn't have been surprised since he had walked all the way from France while I had ridden. Luc told me the 18th Regiment had been assigned to the Third Corps under the command of Marshal Ney.

I was afraid Luc would get swallowed up in the mass of men. Luc's birthday was in June and while I wasn't sure what day the calendar read, I had brought his present along with me. I couldn't be sure when I would see him again. I handed him a small compass that was also a sundial. "I wanted you to have this in case you get lost and want to know what time it is."

Luc smiled and thanked me. "It would be hard to get lost with a crowd like this," he joked. It was so good to see him. We talked about father and the Gerrards and wondered what they were doing. All too soon, we had to say our goodbyes. We hugged and made each other promise to take care of ourselves before we parted ways.

It was obvious by now that we weren't going to Spain or England and most rumors focused on an invasion of Russia and then on to India. Merrien appeared nervous about these rumors. He didn't trust many of the foreign soldiers who were our allies. "We may end up fighting them just to get back to France," he said.

The thing that worried him most, though, was the Russian soldier. He had seen them before on various campaigns, and though the French always won, he blamed that on the incompetent Russian officers. "The Russian soldier," he said, "is the toughest soldier we'll ever fight. They don't care if they live or die. They'll fight until you kill them or give up trying."

The farther we got, the harder it was getting to find food for us and the horses. We had travelled beyond the last supply depots and there was nowhere to buy what we needed. There were many days when we all went hungry.

Chapter 16 - The Edge of Russia

By now, we were heading almost due north. The plains began to give way to trees, and the roads became crowded as the Grande Armée converged on our destination.

With the relentless sun beating down, hunger and the heat were all I thought about. I didn't know where we were going, or what it would be like when we got there, but it had to be better than this.

It was the third week of June when we arrived at a place called Kaunas. We were near the Nieman River, but guards were posted to keep us away from the river so we wouldn't be seen from the other side. As we travelled through Europe, there had been no attempt to conceal our presence, but now, we were attempting to hide the largest army anyone had ever seen. This added to the air of anticipation that could be felt throughout the camp.

I heard that on the other side of the river was Russia and Napoleon was negotiating through diplomats with the Russian emperor, Alexander. If negotiations failed, we would cross the river and invade.

We were ordered to unload our wagons at the ammunition depot and then head a short distance west into the forest where trees were being cut. We hauled freshly cut boards to the bottom of the hill that hid us from the river. We unhitched the teams, leaving the wagons loaded. Finally, the horses could get a much needed rest while we waited to see what would happen next.

A few days later, Merrien told us we had to be ready to move the wagons to the river after sunset. It seemed that Emperor Alexander had not agreed to Napoleon's terms. Three bridges were to be built in secret so the army could begin crossing at dawn and surprise whoever was waiting on the other side.

Once it was dark, we harnessed the teams. Guides came to lead the wagons over the hill and down to the river. We were told to keep as quiet as possible although we could hear the army's engineers at work near the banks driving posts into the river bed. We unloaded the planks as quietly as possible. As we started back to camp with our empty wagon, an officer came running up to us.

"You there!" he said in a loud whisper. I was surprised to see him pointing at me.

"Come with me, we need you," the officer said. I looked at Merrien, who shrugged, and I jumped down and followed the officer along the bank of the river. As we walked, he explained that they needed someone light who could walk out onto something called a balk.

He told me that boats, or pontoons, were launched upstream and drifted down into place where they were held by an anchor. Once the pontoon was in position, a long piece of wood, the balk, would be extended out to it from the bridge 20 feet away. It would be my job to cross over on the balk and secure it to the pontoon. I gulped but didn't say anything. I was afraid to tell him that I did not know how to swim.

We walked out onto the first bridge, which extended about 40 feet into the river. I worked with an energetic man named Francois. He was so confident and reassuring that I began to feel less panicked. First, he showed me how to lash the balk to the pontoon. Once we had done this, men carried out shorter planks, called chesses, to lay across the balks to form the bridge surface. These chesses were lashed down with rope to the balks. Everyone worked together in an efficient and professional manner with minimal communication.

After working for hours, I looked up to find we were near the opposite bank, and the water had become too shallow for the pontoons. One of the men told me to grab the front end of a balk, hop into the shallow water, and walk it in to shore. I was a little annoyed at having to get my feet wet after keeping them dry while crossing the whole river. Still, I did as I was told. As I walked up onto the shore, he said, "Congratulations, you are the first Frenchman on enemy soil."

I looked down at my feet, then quickly up the bank to see if anyone was defending against our invasion. To my relief, no one was there. At the far end of our bridge, I could see cavalry drawn up waiting to cross.

As the cavalry started across, I climbed into a boat heading the other way. The engineers watched the bridge bobbing under the weight of the passing horses. I heard one of them say cavalry was one thing, but marching soldiers was another. Francois explained that men marching in unison created more stress on the bridge than the uneven pace of the horses. In fact, there would be engineers stationed at the entrance of the bridges reminding all units not to march in step while crossing.

When I arrived back in camp, the teamsters were eating breakfast. They all wanted to know where I'd been. Putting up my hands to quiet them, I proudly proclaimed, "I just built a bridge across the river. I chased the Russian army off and then negotiated peace with the Russian Emperor. After I get some sleep, I'm going to build a bridge across the English Channel and negotiate with King George."

"Oh, go on you rotter," they jeered. "What really happened?"

I explained my duties as a pontoneer and how I had been the first to walk on the far bank. Everyone was impressed.

Merrien told me to get some sleep. In spite of all the noise and activity, I didn't wake until supper. As we ate, Merrien told us that we would be crossing tomorrow so we could ferry ammunition to depots inside Russia.

He also added that he had heard nothing of any battles taking place when our men reached the other side. It looked like our attempts at concealing the army had worked.

Merrien concluded by saying, "We're right on the edge. Once we cross the bridge, we're invaders."

Chapter 17 - Invaders

The next morning, our loaded wagons crossed over the bridge I had helped build. Some of the horses refused to cross at first. The bridges didn't have any side-rails and seeing water so close on both sides caused them to stop on the bank. It took a lot of coaxing and persuading on our part, but we finally got them over.

Our destination was a city called Vilna. Rumor had it that Emperor Alexander had been there on the previous day. We expected that the troops up ahead of us would run into the Russian army before long.

Food was a problem from the start. As in Poland, there just weren't many people living there. That meant no food, not much water, and few places for shelter. Also, we were following a few hundred thousand men and their horses who did not leave much in their wake.

We passed some small villages that had been stripped clean by the advancing army. The thatched roofs had even been taken as fodder for the horses. The peasants who were left ignored us as we rolled by. They had seen enough of the army already.

The days were extremely hot, but the nights were cold. I found myself looking forward to night in order to get away from the heat. But at night, I shivered in my blanket.

A few nights after we had crossed the bridge, a cold rain began. We had already stopped and were tending to the horses when it started. We took shelter under the wagons, but the rain was so hard that the ground was soon soaked.

I sat on my oilcloth and pulled my blanket over me. I was in the middle of the group under our wagon, and that helped me stay warm. Somehow I fell asleep.

In the morning, the rain had stopped, but it was still cool. We came out from under the wagons and started to stretch, but then we stopped. All around us, our horses were lying on the ground. We rushed from horse to horse trying to rouse them, but for some, it was too late. The lack of food, being over-worked, and then, a night of cold rain had been too much.

This was just the start of some very disturbing sights that day. As we made our way along the road, we passed not only more dead horses, but dead men, as well. The men had been suffering under the same conditions: lack of food, over work and then the cold rain without any shelter. They had died where they slept.

For the next hour, I stared straight ahead, not wanting to see what might be alongside the road. I couldn't help wondering if Luc had survived the night. Merrien could tell what I was thinking and said gruffly, "Give it up. Luc's a man now. There isn't anything you can do for him except to take care of yourself."

When we finally reached Vilna, we were told that we would be continuing on to Vitebsk, about 200 miles away, as part of a larger supply train. We were provided with an escort of soldiers. About half the wagons in our train carried food, and we were under strict orders to see that the grain made it to Vitebsk for the cavalry.

We were well behind the army, which had proceeded east. The weather had turned even hotter, and the wagons kicked up an enormous cloud of dust. We tied handkerchiefs over our noses and pulled our hats down as far as we could but it was hard to say if it helped or just made it hotter and more miserable.

There were a lot of men by the side of the road who had fallen behind the army. Sometimes alone and sometimes in groups, I doubted they were making a serious attempt to catch up. Others had dropped behind on purpose to prey upon the stragglers. We had to watch out for them when we stopped for the night. Whether they were looking for food to survive or for other types of loot, a supply train always got their attention. I realized that the escort of soldiers had been provided to guard against our own troops, not the Russians.

Our lack of food for the horses became a problem again. Each morning we found we had lost at least one and often more. Passing the carcasses of dead horses and sometimes men became common, but I never got used to it. As we got closer to Vitebsk, we also began to see more and more discarded equipment by the side of the road.

The heat made our need for water even greater than normal, yet there was little to be found. We were travelling across a great, uninhabited plain, which meant there weren't any wells. Our canteens were often empty.

Each time we came to a stream, there was chaos. Wagons would be pulled to the side of the road, and men with canteens and buckets would crowd the banks turning it into a muddy mess. Once the horses had been watered, the wagons would try to get back onto the road, but this would cause a terrible jam. Men argued, officers shouted and the whole column slowed to a crawl until things could be sorted out.

It was early August by the time we arrived at Vitebsk. Our wagons had been spread out along the column, and Merrien was anxious to see if we had all made it. Unfortunately, some of our men, horses and wagons were unaccounted for. There were reports of wagons belonging to our unit abandoned along the road, but nobody could say what had happened to the drivers.

The main body of the army was there, but Ney's Corps had gone off in an attempt to find and engage the enemy. Even taking into account that some divisions were elsewhere, I could tell the ranks were thinner than back in June. Though we hadn't fought a battle, Merrien pointed out that disease, desertion and want of provisions were taking a terrible toll on the army.

Chapter 18 - Looking for a Battle

Napoleon thought he had caught the Russian army at Vitebsk and prepared for a decisive battle. But, the next morning, he found that the Russians had slipped away during the night leaving their campfires burning as decoys.

The rumors about the Russian army and why they hadn't stood and fought swirled around. Some said the Russian commander was a traitor who was working for the French; others said he was afraid of getting his army destroyed and leaving Russia defenseless. Another rumor was that he was buying time, hoping a peace would be negotiated.

The most consistent stories, however, concerned how angry Napoleon was that the Russians would not fight. If he could fight and defeat the Russians, we could all go home. We waited for Napoleon to decide what to do next.

With the army again concentrated in one place, the countryside was being taxed by the large number of men that needed to be fed. If the Russian army wasn't defeated soon, we might be staying here for the winter. It wasn't a happy thought.

We had been in Vitebsk for a few days when orders came to prepare to move. The camp was energized. We were told that the Russian first and second armies were joining up to make a stand less than 100 miles away at Smolensk. The cavalry left immediately. The main body of the army left early the next day.

The supply train travelled in the rear, as usual, with many stragglers in amongst us. We saw men and horses lying dead by the road at an increasing rate. The enthusiasm of heading to battle soon wore off.

There was a new desperation as well. Near the end of the second day, we heard a single shot away from the column. Fearing that an attack was starting, everyone looked in that direction, but there were no more shots. An officer ordered some soldiers to go off and investigate where the shot had come from. That night, we heard that it was a French soldier who had shot himself.

Conditions were so bad for some of the men they had decided they couldn't go on. The next day, we heard two more shots. I tried to imagine how horrible the march must be for the men on foot. Those of us with the teamsters were able to ride so our lack of food was not so hard on us. Also, we were not facing the prospect of a battle at the end of the grueling march. I couldn't help wondering about the dead soldiers' families back home and how they would never see them again here on this earth.

I wasn't too worried about Luc shooting himself, but he must have been suffering like everyone else. I don't know if Merrien could see what I was thinking or not, but he began to tell me how in an army so big, there were always a wide range of circumstances. He told me about a time when he had talked to another veteran from a different regiment that had fought in the same campaign. Merrien said he reminisced about a particularly easy time he'd had while the other remembered only misery. Merrien then related the horrors of a specific battle, and his fellow soldier talked about the glorious experience he'd had in that same engagement.

"So you see," Merrien concluded, "The men up at the front of the column might be dining on fine food and champagne and riding in carriages while we in the back are suffering. You never know."

It was now almost the middle of August. The horrible heat continued and the dust from the road covered everything. To add to the misery, we were harassed by flies, mosquitoes and even wasps. Merrien let me drive to take my mind off of it, and I continued to drive until we reached the outskirts of Smolensk.

As we got closer to the city, we heard musket fire, but were too far away to see anything. I begged Merrien to move closer, but he said that parts of the army were still arriving so it must just be a preliminary skirmish. Sure enough, the firing stopped after a few hours.

As Merrien had predicted, the rest of the day was spent in positioning the army. When it became clear our wagons would not be moving, Merrien gave me permission to go forward and see what was happening. I promised to stay out of the way and return before night. I took off running in the direction I had heard the firing.

Chapter 19 - Messenger

I came to the top of a hill. Down below was the city. Smolensk was situated in the bottom of a bowl formed by hills on both sides of the Dneiper River. Large, thick walls surrounded the city on all sides. From my vantage point, I could look along the ridge and see officers observing the troops below.

I spotted the flag of the 18th regiment. They were close to the river on the western side of the city. After memorizing where they were in relation to the city and the river, I started down the hill. As I descended, a voice from above me demanded, "You there. Where are you going?"

Thinking I might not be allowed to go down to the troops, I thought fast for an excuse. "I'm going to deliver a message for the 18th Regiment in Ney's Corps," I said with as much self-assurance as possible.

"Then you can carry this message for me, as well," the officer replied decisively. He was seated at a small portable desk surrounded by a group of officers who appeared to be vying for the privilege of standing closest to him. From under his hat, I could see a few wisps of curly red hair. This man was someone very important.

He finished writing and held out the folded paper to me. "Take this to General Razout, commander of the 11th division. Tell him Marshal Ney sends his regards." I held out my hand to take the message. I had just told the legendary Marshal Ney a lie.

"Please deliver this message before the one you were about to deliver," he added while giving me a wink.

I could feel my face turning red as I gave him a quick, "Yes, sir," turned, and raced down the hill. I didn't know what General

Razout looked like or where he was, but I knew the 18th regiment was part of his division, so I headed toward the flag of the 18th.

When I got to the flag, I mustered all of my courage and asked an officer where I could find General Razout. Without saying a word, he pointed to a group of mounted officers under a tree.

I recognized General Razout by his uniform as he sat in the middle of the group. I moved among the horses until I was standing next to him. He was having a casual discussion and ignored me. I cleared my throat and said, "Message for General Razout from Marshal Ney who sends his regards."

That got everyone's attention. I handed the message up to General Razout and started to make my way back out of the group. An officer on the fringe suggested I wait to see if there was a reply to deliver.

If I end up delivering messages back and forth all day, I'd never find Luc. Razout finished reading the message and told his officers they should ride forward and have a look at the wall they were to attack in the morning. Off they went without giving me a word or a glance.

I breathed a sigh of relief and headed back to the 18th who were resting in ranks with their muskets stacked. They had been in the skirmish that morning, and all had powder stains on their faces and hands. I found as I moved through them looking for Luc that some were giddy from the experience while others just sat and stared.

It had been nearly two months since I had seen my brother. When I saw him, I forgot myself and called out "Luc!" while racing over to him. We hugged and then stood looking at each other with big smiles. All at once I realized how much I missed him and how scared I had been that he would get hurt. All the worry of the past months fell away as we talked, and I didn't want it to end.

"Fall in!" came the cry up and down the ranks and men began to stand up and straighten their uniforms before retrieving their muskets from the stacks.

I was frustrated that after waiting for two months, I was only able to see Luc for a few minutes. I didn't care what anyone said, I would find a way to stay closer to him from now on. "I'll come back as soon as I can," I promised as I slipped away.

"Be careful," Luc called after me.

I went behind the formations. An officer had begun to address the men. He said the battle would resume in the morning and this time the city would be taken. This brought on a round of "huzzahs" from the men. He continued saying that they would maneuver into position and stay in formation overnight. As the ranks marched off, I made my way up the hill, taking care to avoid Marshal Ney and his entourage.

Chapter 20 - Smolensk

When I reached the teamster camp, Merrien said the wagons would be moving forward during the battle the next day to deliver ammunition. I settled in and tried to get a good night's sleep, but it was impossible. We had played army as kids, but this wasn't pretend. I was unprepared for the feeling of helplessness that overwhelmed me. Luc could be wounded or killed the next day.

We ate a quick breakfast, harnessed the horses and waited. Our cannons soon began to fire, and after awhile, I could hear the crackle of musket volleys in the distance. Fear shot through me. Luc must be going into action.

I was scared to get too close, but not being able to see what was happening and knowing Luc was there was worse. After an agonizing hour, a messenger came back with orders for an ammunition wagon to go forward. I begged Merrien to let it be ours. Merrien agreed because it gave him a chance to see what the situation was before the next wagon had to go.

When we arrived at the crest of the hill above the city, the sight made me forget all about my fear for a few moments. Down below, on our side of the river, the French army surrounded the southern side of the city. To the north, on the opposite side of the river, I could see the Russian army drawn up on the hills overlooking the city. Some of the Russian cannons were firing in support of their men defending the city.

Our troops were in full parade uniform. The sun shone down and made a splendid sight. I could see the ranks moving forward into the outskirts of the city where they disappeared into the streets before the city wall. Smoke from the muskets and cannons soon hid everything from view.

"Let's go," Merrien said as he flicked the reins. We passed near the spot where I had met Luc yesterday. As we came closer to the walls, I could hear the occasional whistling sound of musket balls flying past us. I also saw a cannonball bounce by on the ground. All I could think about was how Luc was somewhere up ahead.

When we stopped, men ran up to unload the boxes of ammunition. One of them wore the coat of the 18th Regiment.

"I'm going to help," I said to Merrien as I jumped off the wagon and caught up with the man. I didn't want to give Merrien a chance to stop me so I didn't look back.

"Give me one end," I said to the soldier as we started into the village under the shadows of the wall. Before we got very far, we saw French troops heading back our way. We had to turn around.

The wave of soldiers continued to push us along until the officers managed to form the men and stop the retreat. The Russians who were pursuing them headed back toward the city. The cannons on both sides continued to fire but most of the shots flew over our heads.

The men sat down in ranks to rest and tend to their wounds. The soldier and I set down the box and began to pass out the cartridges. I went up and down the ranks handing them out and searching for Luc. Finally, I found him sprawled on the ground, exhausted, but unhurt. His face, hands and sleeves were covered with black powder. He looked up at me blankly.

"How are you fixed for cartridges?" I asked.

"I could use some more," he replied dully.

"Are you all right?" I asked as I filled his box.

He took off his hat and ran his fingers through his sweaty hair. "I sure could use some water," he said. Then he seemed to come out of his daze and asked, "What are you doing here?"

"Is your canteen empty?" I asked, avoiding his question in case he intended to send me away.

"Yeah," he sighed, "Everybody's is."

Anxious to help, I said, "Give it to me, and I'll fill it." Turning to the men around us, I gathered as many canteens as I could carry and headed for the nearby river.

As I hurried along, I noticed that the cannonade and musket fire had stopped. A few minutes later, I was scrambling down the riverbank. There were some artillerymen already there watering their horses. I found a spot and began to fill the canteens. As I filled them, I looked around and froze. On the opposite side of the river were some Russian soldiers leading their horses down the bank.

I looked at the Frenchmen on my side to see what they would do. I was afraid I would be in the middle of a fight. To my surprise, one of the Russian soldiers casually raised a hand and greeted us. We didn't speak Russian and they didn't speak French but the meaning of the gesture was clear.

One of our men pulled out a packet of tobacco, tied it to a rock, and threw it across the river where it was caught by a grateful Russian. The Russian began to search through his haversack until he found a small bottle. He flung his arm forward to throw it to the Frenchman. It must have slipped as it left his hand because it ended up heading straight for me. I let go of the canteens and caught the bottle before it hit the rocks. The men gave me a cheer.

Soldiers on both sides started digging things out of their haversacks to throw across. Seeing that I had sure hands, the Russians directed their throws to me and then motioned which of our men was the intended recipient. When the Russians were finished watering their horses, they gathered together and each contributed something to a cloth sack one of the soldiers held. The sack came flying in a high arc. I stepped back a few feet and caught it. I looked up to see who this bundle was for. The Russians all pointed at me, then raised their fists and cheered. It was for me! I waved my hat and shouted, "Thank you" as the Russians turned and headed away.

When all of the canteens were full, I slung them over my shoulders. Staggering under the weight, I went back to the troops. Luc and the others gratefully gulped down water while I looked through the contents of the bag with amazement. There was a chunk of dark bread, some dried meat, a few coins, a pocket knife and a small silver locket.

"Where did you get those?" Luc asked. Men gathered around as I told the story about the meeting with the Russians down at the river.

"But we were trying to kill them earlier this morning," one man exclaimed.

I thought the whole thing was rather odd, but then I had never been in a battle before so maybe that's the way things worked when everybody stopped to rest.

Chapter 21 - City in Flames

The cannonade began again and the men were ordered to form up. Lieutenant Hebert told me I had to leave so I reluctantly said good-bye to Luc and headed back to our wagon staging area. From there we could hear the battle, but not see it. The cannonade continued until the sun began to set. As night fell, there was an orange glow in the sky. We moved forward to the ridge to see what was going on. As we got closer, we could hear a roaring sound and were stunned at the sight that greeted us.

Down below, Smolensk was burning. Flames were visible throughout the whole city and threw enough light that I could see the fire's glow on the faces around me. Men stood and stared without saying anything. I hoped that our troops were not caught inside the city walls. It didn't look like anyone or anything could survive those flames.

Merrien took me by the shoulder and said, "There isn't anything we can do for them. Let's tend to the horses and get some sleep."

In the morning, the news came that the Russians had abandoned the city and burned the bridges as they retreated to the northern side of the river. Our army was to parade into the city, repair the bridges, and pursue the Russians. Word had it that Napoleon was disappointed that the whole Russian army had not come out of the city to fight, and he hoped to catch them on the northern side of the river.

Because our wagons were now empty, we were ordered forward to help with the hauling of materials to repair the burned bridges. As our wagon rolled through the gates, French troops were marching ahead of us like a conquering army, but no one was there to see them. Everywhere we looked, there were charred buildings and blackened corpses in the streets. I was horrified by what I saw, but couldn't look away. It didn't feel real. Some of the charred bodies had their arms stretched toward the sky as if reaching for something. Some were standing against a wall where they had been burned alive by the flames. They didn't look like people anymore. It was hard to imagine they had been alive just the day before.

When we arrived at the river, we had work to do and that helped get my mind off of what we had just witnessed. I recognized some of the engineers I had worked with on the bridge across the Niemen back in June. We were told to scrounge what useable wood we could find and bring it back for the bridges. I didn't want to go back into the city and face those disturbing sights so I asked if I could stay and help the engineers.

Unlike the bridge I had worked on before, this was not a pontoon bridge. It was made to be permanent and had posts driven down into the riverbed instead of boats for support. Enough wood was brought out of Smolensk to make the repairs and, by mid-morning, Ney's Corps started across.

Merrien found me and motioned me over. "Come on, we're going back to Poland."

"Will we be coming back?" I asked.

"Maybe, but it won't be for a long time."

"Then I'm not going. I can't leave Luc."

"Don't be a fool. There isn't anything you can do here. Come on, the others are ready to go."

"I'm not going," I said with a firm voice.

Merrien looked at me for a long time, then said, "Alright, I suppose I would do the same in your position. Come on, let's get your things. There's a lot I need to tell you in the next few minutes."

As we walked to the wagon, Merrien went over all of the advice he had given me during our time together. We were heading deep into enemy territory and couldn't expect any help. He stressed that I should keep my wits about me. Things can turn from good to bad in a wink and those who think ahead are the ones who survive.

When we reached the wagon, Merrien pulled out my duffel and told me to change into my uniform so I could attach myself to Luc's platoon somehow. If I was in a group, we could all look out for each other.

He shook my hand, and swung up onto the wagon. He reached into his shirt and removed a sheath knife he wore around his neck. "You might need this," he said tossing it to me. Standing there, watching him go under the vast Russian sky, I felt very small and very alone.

Chapter 22 - Moving On

After a few minutes, I wiped my eyes, shook myself out of my daze, and found a place to change into my uniform. I set off over the bridge to catch up with the Third Corps.

The road was filled with troops, horses, and wagons. After a few hours, I heard musket fire up ahead. The pace of the troops on the road quickened. The volleys became more and more frequent. Apparently, it wasn't just a skirmish. Before long the troops were ordered off the road to deploy into a battle line. Across the field, I could see the Russians drawn up in formation firing at our advancing men.

My eyes found the flag of the 18th, and I watched as it moved forward with the rest of the line. I wanted to follow, but my feet wouldn't move. I was scared.

Our line fired twice then advanced. The order was given to fix bayonets. After another volley, our troops surged forward with a yell and crashed into the Russian line. The advance stopped for a moment and then began to fall backwards. I could hear the whistle of musket balls as I had at Smolensk.

Eventually, the retreat was stopped, and the line was re-formed and turned to face the Russians. I could see that the advance had been costly because troops in the rear rank stepped up to fill holes in the front rank. The volleys continued and there were more bayonet charges. All of them were thrown back. The sun was starting to set when the firing ceased.

I moved through the ranks looking for Luc. I breathed a sigh of relief when I finally found him tired, but unhurt. The regiment had been in battle three days in a row. They were covered in dirt and worn out.

The Russians had moved off, and Ney was not inclined to follow them in the night. The order came to camp in place. I told Luc the teamsters had left, and I planned to stay with him.

"This is no place for boys. I can't watch out for you here!" he said angrily.

Stung by being called a boy, I snapped back, "You haven't been watching out for me for the past year!" It was true, but as soon as I saw the hurt look on Luc's face, I regretted saying it.

"Father wouldn't be too happy," Luc replied in a resigned voice.

"Well, he isn't here, and I am," was all I said.

I think Luc was secretly glad to have me there. It probably made him feel grown up to think that he would be looking out for me. Of course, the reason I had stayed behind was to look out for him, but I didn't say that.

It was a warm night so we didn't mind sleeping out under the stars. In the morning, I realized how long it had been since I last ate. I asked whether there would be rations issued.

"We haven't had rations in weeks," Luc told me. "We forage for anything we get, and that hasn't been much." I still had a little of the bread I had gotten from the Russian soldiers so Luc and I shared it.

Men were moving over the battlefield. Most of the wounded had been taken to the aid stations in the rear the night before, but occasionally, a soldier was found alive. This was usually discovered when someone was going through his equipment looking for food or other useful items.

Luc found a backpack on the field. He said it would be easier to carry on the march than my duffel bag. As we transferred my things into it, I tried not to think about the man who had carried it up until yesterday.

Later in the morning, we were ordered to fall in. I was worried about what would happen when this order came. Lieutenant Hebert had let me march with him as an aide in Paris, but I wasn't sure where I would fit in on a campaign.

With so many men gone from the ranks, it turned out that I wasn't the only one who didn't know where he should be. As Lieutenant Hebert worked to sort it out, I strode up to him, saluted smartly, and said, "Henri Carle reporting for duty, sir."

To my relief, a smile came over his face, and he said, "I thought you were back with the baggage train. What brings you here?"

I had to think fast. "I've been assigned by, uh, Major Merrien."

"Major Merrien, eh?" he said with a knowing look. "How about you stay close to me until we get organized?"

When Hebert finished re-forming the ranks, he asked me to take the active duty roster to Colonel de Pelleport, the Regimental commander. My first job. As I handed in the report, I kept reminding myself to act as if I were supposed to be there.

Chapter 23 - Foraging

The column left the battlefield around noon and headed east along the Smolensk-Moscow road. We were following the Russian army, but they were pretty far ahead and apparently didn't feel they should stop and wait for us to catch up. In their wake, they left nothing of use. Houses and crops were burned, bridges had been destroyed, and livestock was gone.

After the excitement of the battles, the march along the dusty road in the heat without any food was brutal. I was used to having my gear stowed in the wagon, and I quickly grew tired under its weight. I found myself wondering where Merrien was and how much he was getting to eat.

The heat caused us to drink our canteens dry by mid-morning, and there were very few places to fill them. When we came to a town, we found the Russians had fouled the water by dropping a dead animal down the well. They weren't leaving anything for us to live on. At night, the sky to the east glowed from the fires of burning villages and fields.

We continued like this for days. As before, we often passed dead horses and men along the road. Our ranks became thinner as more and more men fell behind.

When a halt was ordered to allow the stragglers and supply wagons to catch up, Lieutenant Hebert came to Luc's platoon and announced a foraging expedition for which he needed ten men.

"Come on, Henri," Hebert said, "we'll make a forager out of you."

As we set off to the north, Hebert explained that he believed a Russian nobleman's estate was about fifteen miles from the main road. He hoped it was far enough that the Russians had spared it from destruction.

This was enemy territory and we were a long way from the main body of the army. We had to be on the lookout for danger. It was good to be away from the mass of men, but we felt very alone out there.

Early the next morning, we found the estate. There were large fields to the right and woods to the left and behind the main house. It appeared to be untouched. We approached cautiously, looking in all directions for signs of the enemy.

Hebert left Luc and another man on the road as lookouts while the rest of us approached the large house. As we walked up the lane, peasants began to appear and stare at us. When we ran into civilians, we were never sure of the reception we would get. Some were friendly, some were hostile and some were indifferent. I know it was difficult for them to decide how to behave toward us. If they were friendly, they risked the wrath of their neighbors after we left. If they didn't treat us well, they risked having their possessions stolen and their house burned.

These peasants appeared to be taking the indifferent approach. Hebert walked to the front door and knocked. Nobody answered. One of the peasant men came forward and began speaking in Russian.

Hebert gestured that he wanted food, but the man kept talking in Russian and shaking his head. I looked around and noticed a boy watching us from the corner of the house. I walked over to him.

"What is your name?" I asked.

He didn't respond so I pointed at myself and said, "Henri."

The boy nodded, but did not reply. Next, I said, "food" while making the motion of eating from a bowl. The boy just stared.

I stood there wondering what to do next when I noticed he was staring at Merrien's knife. I had pulled it out from under my vest when we approached the house. It was the only weapon I had. I dug through my backpack and pulled out the pocket knife from the river exchange in Smolensk. The boy's eyes lit up, and he reached out his hand to take it. I pulled the knife back and again made the eating motion. This time, the boy turned and motioned for me to follow him. He led me around back to the open door of a kitchen. Two women working at a table looked up and began speaking rapidly in Russian to the boy. A heated discussion followed and then the boy took a loaf of bread from the table and handed it to me. I handed the knife to the boy and watched his face light up.

The women looked at each other and the younger of the two spoke to me in French. "The masters fled to Moscow when they heard the French army was past Smolensk," she said.

"You speak French?" I asked in surprise.

"Yes, the masters speak French so I've picked it up," she replied.

"We've come for food, and we can pay for it. We won't harm anyone."

I pulled out the silver locket I had gotten in the river exchange and handed it to the young woman.

"I'm going to get my lieutenant," I said.

I walked through the house and opened the front door where Hebert and the peasant were still talking and gesturing. Hebert looked at me in surprise, his mouth open and his hands in mid-gesture.

"I found someone who speaks French," I said leading him back to the kitchen.

I introduced him to the young woman who said her name was Olga. They both blushed.

"We would like to... that is, if you are willing to buy, I mean sell us a wagon and provisions, we would be most grateful," Hebert stammered as he fingered the brim of the hat he was holding.

"We will sell you what we can, but you must not tell anyone."

"We won't say anything," Hebert promised earnestly.

The woman turned to the boy and said something in Russian while motioning toward the stable. The boy led me to the stable and showed me the harnesses and wagon. Then we went to the horse pasture. I pointed out two horses, not the best, but not the worst either, and we rounded them up. I hitched them to the wagon. When we pulled up to the kitchen door, our men were bringing food up from the cellar. It looked like they had never been happier.

When the wagon was just about loaded, Luc came running up looking for Lieutenant Hebert. There were some Russian soldiers at the far end of the field heading our way. The other lookout had taken up a position out of sight in the woods. So far, the Russians did not realize we were there.

While Luc helped secure the load on the wagon, I raced into the house and found Lieutenant Hebert and Olga in the parlor.

"Soldiers are coming across the field," I gasped as I burst into the room.

Olga jumped to the window and looked out. Turning to Hebert she said, "They'll be here in a few minutes."

We hurried back to the kitchen. Olga turned to Hebert and said, "They can't know we willingly sold you these things. You must hit me."

Lieutenant Hebert started to protest saying something about being a gentleman.

Olga cut him off, "Slap me across the face, please."

To my great surprise, Hebert did it. Then he overturned the kitchen table spilling bowls, cutting boards, and utensils everywhere.

I was standing there dumbfounded when he turned and pointed to me and three others and yelled, "Carle, you take the wagon down the road about a mile then hide it in the woods and wait for us." Surprised by his actions, I stood frozen. Hebert shouted, "Go!"

We ran out the door and jumped into the wagon. I snapped the reins, and we headed down the lane. Soon we heard shots being exchanged, and I worried about Luc. Still, I did as Hebert had ordered and continued on for about a mile. By the time we were pulling the wagon out of sight of the road, the firing had ceased.

I was still trying to sort out what had just happened. Why had Olga asked Hebert to hit her? Why had he done it and then wrecked the kitchen? Why hadn't he and the other men followed us out the door?

Lieutenant Hebert and the rest of the men soon joined us. They were breathing hard, but all were there and in good spirits. Hebert joined me on the wagon seat. As we set off he noticed my troubled expression and asked me what was wrong.

I didn't want to question him, but I thought if an officer asked me something, it was like an order and I must answer. Still, I decided to skirt the issue. "Why didn't everyone leave at once?"

"We had to finish ransacking the place and lock the staff in the basement."

Seeing my look of horror, he burst out laughing. I didn't think it was so funny.

"Henri," he laughed, "We did it to help them."

Seeing my confusion, he continued, "If the Russian soldiers thought the household staff had helped us, it would have meant trouble. We had to make it look like the staff put up a fight, and we took the provisions. When the soldiers enter the house to let the staff out, they'll see the place was ransacked."

"Is that why Olga asked you to hit her?"

"Yes, she is a very smart woman," Hebert explained.

I felt stupid for not figuring it out on my own. I had a lot to learn.

Chapter 24 - The Road East

The next day it began to rain. To add to our misery, our wagon full of food had been confiscated upon our return and the provisions distributed throughout the regiment. Fortunately, we had already grabbed some food for our own haversacks.

Besides, we sure had ourselves an adventure. Luc said shooting at the Russians to cover the escape from the manor house was more fun than a big battle. I think Hebert was disappointed because he had to leave Olga behind, and his chances of seeing her again were pretty small.

It rained for the next week, and we had no way to get out from under it. Even at night, we slept in the mud with our coats pulled over our heads. My oilcloth wasn't much help, and after days of being soaked, I shivered all the time. To add to our misery, we had almost nothing to eat and the only water we could find was muddy.

The situation changed quickly, however. The rain stopped and news came that Marshal Murat, the daring cavalry leader, had found the Russians dug into positions across the road a few miles ahead. We halted while Napoleon decided what to do.

It was during this time that I had my first experience with a strange disease that had been eroding the strength of the army since we entered Russia. As the army advanced, men began to fall ill with odd symptoms we did not fully understand. A man named Guy from Luc's platoon began to wander around giggling. It was out of character for him and attempts to settle him down were in vain. Later in the day, he became quiet and complained of a terrible headache. By night, he seemed recovered and was joking about his earlier symptoms.

In the early morning hours, however, we were awakened by his moaning and complaints of pain in all of his joints. Lieutenant Hebert told Luc and another man to take Guy to the hospital that had been set up near our temporary camp. When Luc returned, he told of the terrible conditions there.

"I wouldn't call it a hospital," Luc said, "The men have no roof, straw or blankets. There's only one doctor and the stench is unbearable. We were told to lay Guy between two men who were probably dead or will be soon. He took the place of a man who had been dragged away by the ankles." We never saw Guy again.

Orders were given for us to hold roll call and be ready to move into position against the Russians. Lieutenant Hebert told me to stick close to him. He said there would be a lot of maneuvering before the battle began. There would be time for me to get out of the way before the fighting started.

The roll call revealed we were missing about half of the men who had started the campaign in our company. Hebert asked that I take the report to the regimental Colonel. I had delivered a number of messages and reports to Colonel de Pelleport so he was getting used to seeing me.

After I turned in the report, I lingered a little to see what I could hear. The Colonel was ranting about a frontal assault. I heard him talking about a weak left flank "yet he is proposing a full frontal assault!" I assumed "he" was Napoleon. These comments about our regiment's role in the upcoming fight worried me.

Of course, I didn't know anything about the Russian fortifications or how many men or cannons they had. Still, a frontal assault sounded brutal. I didn't want Luc or any of the other men I knew thrown into that. I confided in Lieutenant Hebert the information I had overheard. He didn't seem concerned.

"Plans are always changing. A frontal assault now may turn into a flanking maneuver in the next ten minutes," he explained. "There is no point in worrying about it until it happens."

I had been with the army long enough to know this was true. Orders were issued then changed. Men sometimes had just started complaining about an order when it was rescinded, and they were forced to re-direct their complaints toward its replacement. I decided not to tell Luc or anyone else about what I had heard.

Little did I know that the upcoming battle, referred to as Borodino by the Russians and the Battle of Moscow by the French, would be the bloodiest battle of the campaign. Napoleon himself would call it the most terrible of the fifty battles he had fought.

Chapter 25 - A Personal Showing

As Lieutenant Hebert predicted, there were several changes to the orders that were given the next day. The Third Corps spent the day maneuvering into position to start the battle. This was no easy task as the movements needed to be coordinated with the other corps on either side of ours. There was lots of marching, halting, waiting, more marching, and waiting. The men were hungry, thirsty, tired and frustrated. Many were impatient to start the fight and get it over with. I was hoping the Russians would abandon their positions and continue the retreat.

Around dusk the order was given that all men should be in parade dress for the battle. Everyone set about polishing muskets and buckles and whitening the straps of their belts. The men were still very thirsty so I offered to take a number of canteens and fill them in a stream we had crossed earlier in the day.

After I had filled the canteens and started back, I came across a group of officers including Marshal Ney who called me over.

"Napoleon is going to issue a proclamation to be read to the troops, run over to headquarters and bring it back for me," Ney said as he pointed to a spot behind the lines.

Even though I was weighed down by the full canteens, I ran as fast as I could. This was important. I was being sent to pick up a message from Napoleon. I found a large tent surrounded by officers and soldiers. The sight of so many men and the thought of being so near to Napoleon made me pause. I decided if you act like you know what you are doing, people will listen to you.

I adjusted the canteens and walked with purpose toward the tent. I looked for a clerk of some kind as I pushed my way through the milling crowd. Next to the tent, under the light of two lanterns, sat an officer writing at a field desk.

"I'm here to pick up the proclamation for Ney's corps," I announced in a voice a little too loud.

To my left, I heard someone say, "This one looks a little thirsty," and the soldiers around him laughed at the sight of all my canteens. I turned to look at them and saw a short man in a grey coat with dark, straight hair that fell over his forehead. It was Napoleon. I'd seen paintings of him, but here he was in person. He was standing next to a chair that held a large, framed painting of a young child. Soldiers of the Old Guard, Napoleon's finest troops, were gathered around admiring the painting.

"Come here," the Emperor said holding out a hand to me, "I want you to see this. It is my son, The King of Rome."

The soldiers made room for me, and I walked over to stand in front of the painting. "It just arrived today straight from Paris."

He put one hand on my shoulder and held out his other hand to the painting. "What do you think?"

I didn't know Napoleon even had a son. "I'm sure it looks just like him," I said.

"Ah, a diplomat to be sure," Napoleon laughed. "Someday he'll be in the army, just like you, but for now, he is too young to witness his first battle." Turning to an aide, he said, "Take it into my tent where he won't see."

He then dropped his hand from my shoulder and hurried into the tent. The officer behind the desk called out, "I have the proclamation for the Third Corps."

I went to pick it up, and the officer said, "He's feeling a little under the weather and sometimes needs to excuse himself to use the latrine," as way of explaining the sudden end to my meeting with the Emperor.

His voice sounded familiar. I looked closer, "Lieutenant Faber!" I exclaimed.

"It's Captain Faber now, Henri. Nice to see you," he smiled. I hadn't seen him since leaving Camp Arcola. He looked at my uniform and said, "I see you are with the 18th now. You'll do well there."

By now, a number of nearby officers were looking at us so he added, "Better not keep Marshal Ney waiting."

I took the folded proclamation in my hand, gave him a quick smile and headed off. Ney wasn't hard to spot, but he was hard to catch up with as he rode back and forth, encouraging, adjusting, redeploying and making himself visible to the men. I caught his eye by waving the proclamation over my head.

Ney rode over. As he took the proclamation, he asked, "Did you see the portrait of the King?" with a sly smile.

"Yes, sir," I answered. "Emperor Napoleon showed it to me himself."

Ney raised his eyebrows. "Well, a personal showing, I'm impressed," turning to his aides, he said, "This young man may be a marshal by morning."

Ney turned back to me and touched the front of his hat, "Thank you for your service," he said before riding off.

I rejoined the regiment and distributed the canteens. "What took you so long?" the men were asking.

"If I told you, you wouldn't believe me," was all I said.

We were soon called to attention, and Marshal Ney himself read the proclamation to our regiment. In his loud and clear voice, he began: "Soldiers! This is the battle that you have looked forward to so much!" That wasn't the case for me. The images of Smolensk and the corpses along the road drifted through my mind. I had seen enough of battles and death. As I brought my attention back to Marshal Ney, he finished reading Napoleon's words, "... let people say of you: 'He was at that great battle fought under the walls of Moscow!'"

The men gave three "huzzahs." On the hills across from us, we could see the campfires of the Russian army. Some men wondered aloud whether the enemy would be there in the morning.

They were.

Chapter 26 - Borodino

The Russians had chosen to build their fortifications across the Smolensk-Moscow road at the village of Borodino, seventy miles west of Moscow. We didn't realize what we were facing that morning of 7 September 1812. It was drizzling as we stood up from where we had lain for the night and stretched out the stiffness. It was still dark, but none of us could sleep any longer.

Just after sun-up, the first French cannon fired and the shot arched over our heads on the way to the Russian lines. More cannons joined in and then the Russian batteries began to respond. We were within range of the Russian guns and were eager to begin the attack.

When the shots began to fall among the men, Lieutenant Hebert told me to go back out of range and watch the battle from a safe distance. I knew there was no use arguing so I reluctantly turned to head away. Once out of his sight, I doubled back and stationed myself behind the ranks of the 18th. I was determined to share the fate of Luc and the other men.

We had been told we would be attacking one of two earthen fortifications in front of us. These fortifications were called "flèches." They had "V" shaped walls with the point toward us and the open end facing away. We were to attack the northern flèche while troops to our right would attack the southern.

To stand in formation while being fired at with cannons was terrifying. The officers did their best to offer encouragement and could be heard saying, "Steady, men, steady," over and over.

Above the din of artillery fire, the order was given to fix bayonets and advance. The men cheered, but a wave of fear swept through me. I was afraid my legs would give way, but I stumbled forward behind the rear rank.

The sounds were deafening. The men cheered, the drums played, and the cannons boomed. Muskets crackled as the Russians in the flèches fired on us, but we were still out of range. Our line of troops advanced at a steady pace down a slight hill. At the bottom was a small stream that we waded in formation. The line wavered a little as we came out the other side and climbed the opposite bank. Men struggled to maintain their pace. Officers shouted, pushed, and threatened in order to keep the ranks in a straight line as they moved over the uneven ground. We halted and fired a volley, then re-loaded and resumed the advance.

As the mass of troops moved forward, cannons from the flèche tore holes in our line with rounds of grapeshot. Four or five men at a time would fall as the shot ripped though our tightly packed ranks. Too shocked to scream, the men could only gasp as they collapsed. The sound the balls made reminded me of a rock landing in mud as arms and legs were torn away splattering my uniform with blood. Soldiers from the rear ranks stepped over the fallen soldiers to fill in the gaps. The assault was taking a heavy toll.

I caught glimpses of the dirt wall of the flèche, and I knew that there must be a ditch in front of the wall. By now I was so scared I could hardly breathe, but I had nowhere to go. Everywhere I looked were men, horses and smoke. I had to keep moving forward.

When we were almost to the flèche, the command to "charge" was given. With a cheer, the line surged forward, and the first two ranks of men went into the ditch in front of the flèche. They began to scramble up the earth wall while the Russian soldiers fired down on them. The third and fourth ranks fired into the flèche until the men of the first two ranks had either reached the top of the wall or had fallen back into the ditch wounded or dead. I followed the second group as they too charged into the ditch and struggled up the wall.

Somehow, I reached the top unharmed. When I looked over, I couldn't believe what I saw. The men inside the flèche were fighting in a desperate struggle, stabbing with bayonets and swinging their muskets like clubs. Bodies were everywhere. I slid back down into the ditch and huddled there among the dead and wounded. Soon, our troops began to pour back out of the flèche. I scrambled out of the ditch and started to run with the retreating soldiers. The officers halted the retreat after we had crossed the stream.

Marshal Ney appeared and began shouting and waving his sword. The command to advance was given, and we headed back to the flèche. Each time a wall of lead shot out from the flèche, our lines would suffer heavy losses, but again, the men went into the ditch and then up over the wall before being pushed out and back across the stream.

Some of the men sank down in place, too exhausted to stand. Uniforms that had been worn on parade in Paris a few months before were now torn and covered with dirt and blood. Men's faces were smeared with gunpowder and sweat. Marshal Ney was shouting that we needed reinforcements and rode off to the rear.

The men drained their canteens, and some risked the fire from the flèche to go forward and refill them at the stream. Davout's men on our right had been thrown back as well. We all waited for whatever would come next.

When Ney returned, he conferred with his officers, and then rode up and down the line, waving his sword and shouting for us to move forward. Our men advanced once again. The front ranks were soon crossing the ditch and climbing the wall. As before, the Russians in the flèche were firing down on them, but our line kept climbing.

Almost at the top, our assault began to waver as more Russians appeared and met our attack. I stepped back from the edge of the ditch. I expected our line to be repelled before we entered the flèche.

Time seemed to stand still. The sky was black with smoke. Despite the din of the battle, with the artillery barrage so intense it sounded like one long rumble, I could see and hear what happened next with perfect clarity. As our men began to slide back down the side of the earthen wall, Lieutenant Hebert made it to the top. He held his sword high in the air and shouted, "It is ours, men! Let's take it!" Then Hebert reached down and hoisted the man closest to him to the top of the wall by his cross belts. With a yell that made the hair on my neck stand up, the men surged up and over the top of the wall. Lieutenant Hebert disappeared down into the flèche.

When our attack was not immediately repulsed, I climbed up the wall and dropped down over the top. The scene was just as wild and savage as before. I watched helplessly with my back to the wall.

A Russian cannon sat abandoned to my right on an earth platform. An officer shouted to some nearby men to turn the cannon around and use it to help push the Russians out. The men turned the cannon toward the enemy, but had no idea what to do next. Without thinking, I ran forward and picked up the ramrod that lay on the ground. I found the ammunition chest under some bodies and two of the improvised artillerymen carried it behind the gun. I instructed one of them on how to fill the touchhole with priming powder as I had been taught back at Arcola.

I rammed powder and a ball down the barrel and then turned to aim the gun. I elevated the cannon's muzzle so the shot would fire over the men fighting in front of me and would fall into the ranks of Russians advancing to reinforce their comrades. I shouted the command to fire and turned out of the way as flames shot out of the barrel.

I called for more powder and shot, and I rammed down charge after charge, firing over and over. The blast from the cannon made my ears ring, and it temporarily blocked out the noise of the battle raging around me. I could see that we were in danger of being pushed out of the flèche again. In front of us, our men had moved away from the mouth of the cannon exposing the advancing Russian line.

I called for one more charge of powder and grapeshot. I lowered the muzzle of the cannon to fire directly into the line of Russian soldiers who were now only a few yards away. We were able to fire the shot before the Russians were at the gun.

I couldn't think about anything, only react. I used the thick wooden ramrod to push one Russian aside as he came toward me. Soon there were so many men pressed in together that I was pinned up against the gun carriage. I don't know how long it took, but our men finally pushed the Russians out of the flèche and into retreat. I sank down where I was, exhausted, and gave in to the urge to close my eyes.

I became aware of someone on horseback standing very close. I opened my eyes to see an officer looking down at me.

"Just like your father," he said. He raised his sword and slowly swept it toward the ground in a salute. He looked familiar, but who was he? Then it all came together. It was Major Briere, the recruiting officer who knew my father and saluted him on the day Luc and I went away with the army.

I pulled myself to my feet and said, "Thank you, sir." Now was my chance to find out more. "How do you know my father?" I asked

"We served together under General Rochambeau in America. When our unit attacked a British redoubt at Yorktown, your father was the first one over the wall. It was by his example that the men were inspired to take that redoubt. When it looked as if the British were mounting a counter attack, he wheeled a cannon around and fired it until he was wounded. Those wounds cost him a brilliant military career."

Major Briere continued, "I thought there was some of your father in you that day you tried to enlist. I was right." With that, he raised his hand to the brim of his hat and rode off.

Chapter 27 - Aftermath

As I watched Major Briere ride away, my thoughts turned to Luc. I was surrounded by bodies, some dead, some wounded. A feeling of despair swept over me, and I had to fight the urge to sit down and give up. Further up the hill behind the flèche, I saw the flag of the 18th, and I broke into a run.

I called for Luc as I moved through the men lying or sitting around the flag. Nobody paid attention to me. I became more and more frantic. If I didn't find him here, I would have to go back to the flèche and look for him among the shattered bodies.

At last I saw him sitting up at the sound of his name. I rushed over and hugged him. He wasn't wounded, but he was exhausted. As soon as I let go, he slumped back to the ground. Looking around at the disorganized mob, I asked, "Where's Lieutenant Hebert?"

Luc pulled himself up to a sitting position once more, and said he had last seen Hebert in the flèche. The only people there now were dead or wounded. "Come on," I said, helping Luc to his feet, "we've got to find him."

As we headed to the flèche, I nearly stepped on Lieutenant Hebert. His white vest was covered with blood. He was having trouble breathing, and it was hard to tell if he even recognized me. When I knelt down beside him, I could see part of his insides through a gaping hole in his side. I gasped and turned away. Luc told him we were taking him to a hospital, but Hebert weakly whispered, "Take someone else."

"No," I said, "you need help. You have to live."

Lieutenant Hebert just closed his eyes. I looked at Luc, but he shook his head. He understood the situation better than I did. I saw two stretcher bearers and asked them to come take an officer to the hospital. They looked at Lieutenant Hebert and said it was too late.

I didn't want to believe them, but when I knelt down next to him again, I could tell he was no longer breathing. I lowered my head and cried. Luc pulled me into an embrace, and I buried my face in his coat. I didn't try to hold back the tears.

We sat that way for a long time without saying a word. A few men walked among the bodies, poking here and there, looking for things they could use. Finally, Luc looked up at the darkening sky and said we should find a place to sleep.

We walked as far as we dared from the carnage on the field and lay down next to each other under the same blanket. We gave in to our overwhelming weariness. As the sounds of the wounded died away, we slept.

In the morning, we found the remains of the regiment assembling around the flag. We looked for members of Luc's platoon, but couldn't find any. A grizzled sergeant spotted us and said, "Which platoon were you in?"

"Lieutenant Hebert's, in Captain Blanc's company," Luc answered.

"Form there," the Sergeant said pointing to a spot, "My name is Sergeant LaGrand. I'll be your new platoon leader. There aren't enough lieutenants left."

LaGrand? I thought he looked familiar. He was the Sergeant who had taken our recruiting party from Reims to Camp Arcola. It was like seeing an old friend.

Noting that Luc did not have his gun, LaGrand asked, "Why don't you have your musket?"

"I lost it in the battle, sir," Luc said looking down.

"A soldier never 'loses' his gun. It has to be pried out of his dead hands," LaGrand growled. "Do you understand?"

"Yes, sir," Luc said with a stronger voice.

"As long as you are a soldier in this army, you will never be caught without your weapon again. I want you to eat, sleep and do your daily business with it. Do you understand?"

"Yes, sir!" Luc responded, standing at stiff attention and looking straight ahead. "It won't happen again, sir."

"Good, now go find a musket and as many cartridges as you can carry. Make sure they're Russian cartridges, they're better than ours."

The Sergeant turned his attention to me. Noting my uniform and my age, he asked, "Are you part of this regiment?"

"Yes, sir," I answered as convincingly as I could.

"Where is your gun?" he asked.

"I'm a messenger," I said.

"We don't have messengers anymore. Go find a musket and cartridge box. Look in the northern flèche. There was a cavalry charge there so you can find a carbine. They're shorter and will fit you better."

He saw me hesitate and added, "Don't worry, the men there won't be needing them anymore. May their souls rest in peace. Now go." With that, he turned his attention to another straggler who had shown up.

I thought Sergeant LaGrand hadn't recognized us, but then he called after me, "Make sure you stay away from any chicken coops." He remembered us after all. LaGrand had protected Luc and me the night we threw chickens into Gaston's shed. I had the feeling having him with our platoon would be a good thing.

In the flèche we had captured, there were plenty of muskets and equipment but no carbines. "He told me to look in the northern flèche," I said to Luc, "but I don't remember seeing a cavalry charge." I looked north and saw another flèche we hadn't known about before the battle. We had actually attacked the middle flèche. I was learning that in war, there is always something unexpected.

It turned out that there were three flèches instead of the two we had been told about before the battle. When we got to the northern flèche, we found we weren't the only ones looking through the aftermath. Other soldiers, Russian villagers, and even a priest were there.

I spotted a few carbine muskets but feared taking them from a dead man's hands. Luc didn't hesitate. He grabbed one, and said, "Now, let's get you a cartridge box."

I held the carbine in my hand. It was shorter than the musket Luc had found for himself. When I rested the butt end on the ground, the end of the barrel came up to just below my shoulder. The cavalry carried them because the shorter barrels made them easier to handle and shoot from a horse.

Luc slipped a cartridge box off one of the bodies, shortened the strap, and hung it over my shoulder. He raided Russian cartridge boxes until both of ours were full. Properly equipped, we headed back to our new platoon.

Sergeant LaGrand addressed us: "Men, we're a long way from home, and we may not be heading back for a long time. As morbid as it sounds, I want you to check all your clothing and equipment. If you need anything, go find it on the battlefield. Take it with respect, it once belonged to a brave man who would have wanted you to have it. I wouldn't count on being issued any new clothing or equipment until we get back to Poland. Only God and Napoleon know when that will be, and it's possible Napoleon hasn't even told God yet."

He continued, "Once you've got what you need, get to know the men in your platoon. You'll all have to work together if we want to see home again."

Chapter 28 - To Moscow

None of us had eaten in the past day, but by searching the haversacks that were left on the field, we cobbled together a breakfast. As we ate we tried not to think about where it had come from.

Sergeant LaGrand had us re-load our packs. Everything was taken out and examined and then put back with the heavier items on the top. Even our blankets were re-rolled tightly to fit the packs better. When we put our packs back on, they somehow felt lighter. Sergeant LaGrand's experience was already making a difference.

Soon, an order came for us to continue the march to Moscow. Rather than attacking us in our weakened state, the Russians had retreated. They were hurting too. We began the march in good order, but as the day went on, the fatigue caught up with us and some men in our platoon began to lag behind. LaGrand would have none of it. He prodded, cajoled, and threatened the stragglers until they caught up again.

We went on like this for days, exhausted, with little chance to rest. It seemed like we just had a few hours of sleep each night before we were up and moving again. LaGrand would encourage us by saying things like, "I think I can see Moscow from here," and, "There is a bed with your name on it up ahead."

We all expected another battle. Despite what Napoleon's proclamation had said, the battle at Borodino was not fought under the walls of Moscow. We felt sure the Russians would stand at least once more before we could claim it as our own.

We were exhausted and underfed. Each step was an effort. Covering the 70 miles to Moscow was proving to be battle enough. We often passed stragglers who had sat down and given up. Despite the threat of what the Cossacks would do to a single soldier or small group, these men just couldn't go on.

Our platoon stayed together better than most, and we owed it to Sergeant LaGrand. The thing that kept us going was the thought that in Moscow we could eat our fill of anything we wanted. LaGrand played this up by saying, "I smell bread baking" or, "I hope we make it in time for supper."

In the morning of the seventh day, the column came to a halt. This often happened in bad weather when a wagon or gun carriage needed to be pulled from the mud. But this was a clear day, and the road was in good condition. Something big must be going on. The men began to leave the road and press forward with excitement.

A hilltop ahead was crowded with men standing motionless. We were anxious to see what was so interesting and moved forward with the rest. Officers were riding amongst the crowd ordering the men to reform their units, but they weren't having much success. When I reached the top of the hill, any thought of hunger or fatigue vanished from my mind.

There, down below, lay Moscow. It was a city ringed with a wall made of reddish stone behind which rose the spires and domes of what looked like hundreds of churches. Although not the capital, Moscow was the spiritual heart of Russia, and we believed that its capture would lead to the surrender of our enemy.

Almost as stunning as the sight of this great city was the fact that the Russian army was nowhere to be seen. The city stood still and quiet under the golden September sun.

The voice of LaGrand broke me from my trance, "Come on, it's just a big town with lots of churches, move along."

We headed back down the hill toward the road. The column re-formed, but didn't move. We were to wait until Napoleon had looked over the situation.

The fact that the Russian army wasn't there made us all feel uncomfortable. Was it a trap? Were they circling behind us? We couldn't believe they would abandon the city without a fight.

In the evening we were told that some of our cavalry had entered the city and found only a few inhabitants. Our orders were to camp in place and prepare to enter the city in the morning in full parade dress.

Even though we had nothing to eat, the talk that night was not of food. Everyone was planning how they would spend the fortune of loot they would find. Since I was only fourteen, my wants and desires were much simpler. I was hoping for a good meal and a full night's sleep. Many of the men on the campaign, however, had expected to become rich with plunder long before this, but the country was so barren that there had been nothing to gain. The thought of the riches in Moscow made these men delirious.

Chapter 29 - The Empty City

When the drums sounded in the morning, there was no difficulty in rousing the men. We stepped out with enthusiasm. Sergeant LaGrand slowed our pace by saying, "Relax, the city isn't going anywhere."

I knew each man was thinking he had to get into the city first to get the best things for himself. Luc and I exchanged glances. Luc let out a strange giggle. I thought maybe he was caught up in the euphoria of the moment and anticipating some loot of his own.

The road led us through some trees and when we emerged, we could see the sun shining on the golden domes of the city. The pace quickened again. Luc made another giggling sound and then proceeded to talk to himself. Some of the men around us were talking and nudging their neighbors.

The order came to fix bayonets, and we were soon passing through a gate in the wall. The sounds of drums echoed off the walls as the musicians passed through. We emerged from the shadows and into the sunlight. The further we marched, the more the men began to look around and murmur. Even though the streets were lined with houses, nobody appeared to greet or oppose our army.

Good order was maintained as long as our column was moving, but once we stopped, men melted away from the ranks. Soon, the only ones left from our platoon were Luc, Sergeant LaGrand, and me. LaGrand shook his head and sighed, "While the rest of the army is off making its fortune, we should secure some quarters."

LaGrand motioned for us to follow him, but Luc bent over and complained of a bad headache and aching back. I thought it was from the effects of hunger and marching for weeks on uneven roads, but LaGrand looked more concerned, "How long have you felt this way?" he asked.

"Since we entered the city," Luc said.

"Let's get you someplace you can lie down," LaGrand said as he took Luc under one arm.

We walked up the steps of a nearby house. LaGrand knocked on the door, but nobody answered. He knocked once more and then tried the door. It was unlocked.

After a few minutes, he re-appeared in the doorway and told us to come inside. "We'll take Luc upstairs," he said. We helped Luc, who could barely stand, up the steps and into a large, well-furnished bedroom.

After settling him in the bed, LaGrand headed downstairs to look for something to eat. I looked out the large windows at the street below. I could see soldiers carrying clothes, boxes, even furniture from the surrounding houses.

Sergeant LaGrand re-entered the room with a bottle of wine, some cheese, and meat in his hands. "We're in luck," he said, "there is some food in the basement kitchen, and they even left a servant behind. We've occupied the house of some sort of nobleman who's fled the city like everyone else."

We tried to rouse Luc to eat, but he just gave us a sleepy look and closed his eyes again. LaGrand and I ate ravenously.

When we had finished, Sergeant LaGrand said we must gather provisions. While the rest of the army was looking for jewels, silver and gold, they would overlook food. Eventually, though, their stomachs would demand to be fed. We needed to stock up before that happened. There was no telling how long we would be in the city.

Luc was sleeping when Sergeant LaGrand and I headed out into the street. On the sidewalk, there were pieces of furniture, candlesticks, spinning wheels, clothes, and just about any other household thing imaginable. All of these had been stolen and then rejected for better loot by the soldiers.

LaGrand and I headed further into the city, and we found an empty butcher shop. "This place doesn't look like it was looted," he said. "I bet they just hid everything before they left." LaGrand suggested we search carefully. Sure enough, we found a trap door in the floor that led down to a storeroom with all kinds of hams, beef and sausages.

When we went back up the steps to look for a cart, a few soldiers burst in the front door and saw us. "Empty," said LaGrand sadly as he closed the trap door. The soldiers' shoulders sagged as they turned and headed back out to the street.

"That was close," LaGrand said, "grab the butcher's cart and that canvas to cover it so we can get this back to the house."

Once the cart was loaded, LaGrand said, "Walk like you are on a mission with orders from Napoleon himself. Don't let anyone stop or question us."

Remembering Sergeant LaGrand's instructions, I kept my eyes straight ahead and walked briskly with the cart. When we got to our street, we could see a large group of soldiers milling about. They weren't part of our regiment so LaGrand turned to the alleyway that ran behind the houses.

Unfortunately, we didn't know which house was ours from the back. As we walked along, trying to estimate how far down the block it was, some of the soldiers from the street appeared at the alley entrance and called for us to stop. We didn't look back, so the men quickened their pace and shouted threats. A door in front of us opened, and a woman waved us in. We pushed the cart through the doorway and barred the door behind us.

"Henri, I haven't had the chance to introduce you to Sophie, the maid of this household," said LaGrand as Sophie curtsied.

I bowed my head. Sophie reminded me a lot of Beatrice Mahovlich, pleasant and friendly, but older and a little more plump. Sophie smiled and said in broken French that we had better get the contents of the cart down to the cellar. As we unloaded the cart, Luc appeared and said he felt well enough to help. We looked at him in surprise and told him to go rest some more, but he insisted he was better.

I looked around the basement kitchen and could see there was plenty of food there. What a welcome change from the march. In fact, Sophie had a stew cooking and produced three bowls into which she ladled a generous serving for each of us.

As we ate, LaGrand said we needed to be careful with the supplies. It was only mid-September, and they might have to last us through the winter. He suggested we go back out, find more food, and round up the men from our platoon.

With a hot meal in our stomachs for the first time in weeks, we pushed back from the table. Luc said he wanted to join us. We picked up our guns and headed out the back door, taking the cart along.

Out on the street, we could smell smoke. LaGrand sniffed the air and muttered about the careless fools in our army who must have started a fire by accident.

LaGrand told us to keep an eye out for anything we could find to eat or that might be useful later. "I keep hearing about the cold Russian winter. At the first cold snap, everyone in the army will be looking for hats, gloves and overcoats. If you see any now, grab them."

Rounding the corner, we saw some of the men from our platoon carrying a sofa. LaGrand stopped in the middle of the street, put his hands on his hips and looked at them with a "what now?" look. Upon seeing LaGrand, the men stopped and looked at each other sheepishly, then put down the sofa and stood at semi-attention.

"That's better. We've got a house on the street where we, ah, dismissed, earlier today. Our unit name is carved in the door. I want you to work on gathering food and useful items," LaGrand said looking at the sofa. The men each slid a half-step further away from the embarrassing loot. "When you're done with that, meet us back at the house."

The men saluted and headed off, leaving the couch behind. LaGrand muttered, "You two are the youngest ones in the platoon, but you have more sense than the rest of them put together."

By now, the smell of burning wood had become stronger. We could sometimes see black smoke blowing over the tops of the buildings. "Army of fools," LaGrand said shaking his head.

We rounded the corner and almost ran into Captain Blanc, our company commander. After saluting, we noticed the Captain was carrying a bottle of wine in each hand. "Have your men secured lodging?" he asked LaGrand.

"Yes, sir. On the street where we dismissed this morning."

"Very well, carry on," Blanc said as he continued on his way.

After Captain Blanc was out of earshot, LaGrand said to us, "If you see any wine, grab it. That stuff will be like gold in a week."

The sun was shining, and it was a pleasant autumn afternoon. We walked through the captured city with full stomachs. For the first time in months, I was not going to sleep under a wagon or out in the open. Things were going well. I didn't know it then, but this was the best I would feel for a long, long while.

Chapter 30 - By Their Own Hands

S pying a shop with the door standing wide open, LaGrand suggested we see what was inside. It turned out to be a tailor's shop. Bolts of cloth had been scattered around, but it didn't look like much had been taken. Stooping to pick up some heavy blue wool, LaGrand said, "This will come in handy," as he took it outside to the cart.

I found some needles, thread and scissors. I asked where we would pay for these things. LaGrand chuckled and said, "This is known as the army discount. Just put it in the cart."

My eyes widened. I hadn't thought too much about it while we were loading the meat at the butcher shop, but I was used to paying for things. "You'll get over it," LaGrand promised, "If you don't take it, somebody else will. If it makes you feel any better, we can leave a list of what we've taken, and the owner can apply to the army for payment."

After we made the list, we closed the door and headed back by way of the butcher shop to top off our cart. I asked LaGrand about leaving an inventory of what we took. "We'll bring it back later," he replied, "right now, we need to get back to the house."

He had been glancing more and more at the sky, which was now filled with a steady stream of smoke. It was obvious the fire somewhere in the city was becoming larger.

As we walked, I realized Luc had grown quiet, and his pace had slowed.

"Are you all right?" I asked him. He didn't answer, but looked at me with a tight-lipped grin.

"We'll be there soon," Sergeant LaGrand said.

Back at the house, Luc sat down on the steps to the kitchen, "I hurt everywhere," he said.

"Come on," I offered, "I'll help you up to bed."

After we slowly climbed the stairs, I helped Luc into the bed and asked what I could get for him. He couldn't even answer, just moaned.

I ran down to the kitchen to find Sophie. She was ladling out stew for several members of our platoon who had found their way back to the house. "Please come upstairs and see if you can help my brother," I blurted, "He's awful sick, and I don't know what to do for him."

As we headed up the stairs, we heard a pounding on the front door. One of our men, Jean, opened the door with his gun at the ready. After a quick conversation, Jean turned and shouted, "Everybody fall in, the city's on fire, and we've got to put it out."

As the men tramped outside, LaGrand called to me to come down.

"Sophie can take care of Luc," he said, "We need you out there."

We left our muskets and equipment behind and assembled in the street. Some men were hurrying by with buckets, but others were still carrying loot. Captain Blanc called us to attention.

"There are a few houses on fire to the south," he said, "we need you as part of a bucket brigade. It seems that the pumps used to fight fires are all missing."

When he mentioned "bucket brigade," many of the men moaned. But it was the part about the missing pumps that scared me. It seemed like too much of a coincidence that the empty city was on fire with no equipment for putting it out. I feared the Russians had let us into the city so they could burn it to the ground with us inside.

Captain Blanc gave the command, and we moved out as a company. By now, it was dusk and the air was cool. I pulled my uniform collar up and tried to get my mind off of Luc. It wasn't long before the scene we found had my full attention.

We had only gone a few blocks when we could see men in the streets up ahead and hear the sound of a raging fire. The whole block was in flames. Every so often, parts of a roof would collapse, sending up a shower of sparks. The glow of the flames was so bright we could see as easily as in daylight.

Without any pumps and no ready source of water, it was impossible to fight the flames. We stood mesmerized by the scene. A commotion arose behind us, and we turned to find another fire had started in an empty alley we passed by only a few minutes before. As the flames were still small, we had a chance to fight this one. Some men went in search of water. Others took off their coats and began to beat at the flames. A well was found, and I joined the bucket brigade swinging buckets of water down the line to the fire.

It was obvious that this fire had been deliberately set. As soon as it was out, our platoon was ordered to return for our weapons and begin patrolling the streets to catch the fire setters.

Back at our house, I checked on Luc. He was fast asleep, but Sophie said that he had been in terrible pain earlier. I wanted to stay, but I heard my name being called from the street. I squeezed Luc's hand and hurried downstairs.

We were ordered to fix bayonets, and stop anyone we saw on the streets. Our platoon was split into two groups to search each opening and alleyway. Each group moved down the street at the same pace so if we found someone on one side, the rest of our men would be nearby to lend assistance.

By now it was dark, and we didn't have any lanterns. The streets were lined with tightly spaced houses, and the glow of the blaze was too far away to shed light. It would be hard to spot someone until we were right on top of them.

I had been placed in a group with Jean and Serge. When we reached the first alley, Jean told Serge and me to stay at the opening while he searched. As my eyes grew accustomed to the dark, I could see Jean standing at the other end. He came back and reported the alley was clear. Across the street, we could see the others had finished a search on their side as well.

We continued down the street, checking doorways, window wells and alleys while LaGrand and the other men kept up on their side. The street was silent and black, and the tension was high. My hands were squeezing my musket, and despite the cool night air, I was sweating. The thought of the enemy so near was exciting and scary. Especially since I was now armed.

As I switched my gaze from the street to the alley, I caught sight of someone ducking behind a house farther down the street. Or did I? In a whisper, I asked Serge what to do. I don't think he believed I had seen anything so he just waved for me to check it out myself. I began to panic. What if I did find someone? I didn't want to look foolish in front of the men. They were probably already laughing about having a fourteen-year-old boy in the ranks.

I squeezed the musket even tighter and kept walking toward where the shadow had disappeared. Then, something on the ground caught my eye. It was a few pieces of straw. As I bent down to pick it up, I was bowled over by a man bursting out of the alley. As I fell, the man's foot caught on my musket. The barrel swung around and hit me on the head. The gun went off sending the shot harmlessly down the street, but drawing everyone's attention.

Serge and Jean arrived and leveled their bayonets at the man who was sprawled on the brick sidewalk. As I got to my feet, my head hurt from being hit by my own musket and my shoulder from when I hit the ground. I was more embarrassed, though, than anything.

The man on the ground sat up and began blubbering and talking fast while clasping his hands in front of him as if he were praying. Sergeant LaGrand stepped forward and barked, "Enough!" and the man stopped in what seemed like mid-sentence. LaGrand looked around at us and said, "Did anybody understand that?" We all shook our heads. "Where's Stosh?" LaGrand asked.

Stosh stepped forward. He had either been born in Poland, grew up in Poland or had once visited there, we weren't quite sure because he never said very much. We just knew he spoke some Polish, and we had heard Polish was close to Russian. LaGrand asked Stosh to find out what the man was up to out on the streets at night with fires starting all around.

Stosh spoke to the man in a very slow and deliberate way. The man looked at him with a puzzled expression. Stosh tried again. The man began to sob and speak in bursts with his hands still clasped. LaGrand asked what he had said.

Stosh thought for a moment and said, "He was out walking for some fresh air... or he has a chicken in his boot. I'm not quite sure."

LaGrand sighed, and his shoulders slumped.

Stosh was quick to explain, "I grew up in France, my grandparents spoke Polish around the house, and I picked up bits and pieces. Polish and Russian are different languages."

"Never mind," grumbled LaGrand, "search his pockets and look between the houses where he was lurking."

Two men hauled the unfortunate man to his feet while I went back between the houses. In a window well, I found some straw with oily rags stuffed underneath. Meanwhile, Jean was pulling flint and steel out of the man's pocket. "Well, well," LaGrand said as he lightly tossed the flint and steel in his hand. "It looks like the city is burning by their own hands."

Chapter 31 - Winds of Disaster

Many "incendiaries" were caught that night, but the damage had been done. The winds picked up and spread the flames across Moscow. We were fortunate that the wind blew away from our section of the city.

Discipline in many parts of the army had broken down. As a result those units that had managed to stay together were pressed into service around the clock for the next few days to fight the fires where possible and to guard against more fires being set. Guards were posted at intersections to prevent people from moving about the city, and our regiment manned many of the intersections in our area.

With guard duty and snatching sleep whenever I could, I didn't get to see Luc very much. Luc's room had been made into an infirmary, and several more men were now staying there. Luc was in agony, complaining about pain everywhere. When I tried to visit, I wasn't sure he knew I was there. Sophie shooed me away saying there was nothing I could do for him, he just had to rest.

Standing on guard duty, I had lots of time to think. Luc was very sick and there were no doctors to be found. The medical corps was overwhelmed by the casualties from the battle at Borodino. I started to wonder if Luc would ever make it back to see father again. Turning my back to the men on guard with me, I cried softly to myself.

Someone put his arm around me. It was Serge. He told me Sergeant LaGrand wanted me back at the house. We walked together in silence, both knowing the reason I had been sent for. Sophie met me at the door. Her eyes were red and filled with tears. I went upstairs to Luc's bedside.

Luc laid there with his eyes half open and slowly turned his head to me. It didn't look like he was in pain. It looked like he had given up. I grabbed his hand with both of mine and held it tight.

"I love you, Luc," I gasped out in a hoarse whisper. He gave me a weak smile and squeezed my hand. "You'll be all right. You just need rest. Do you want something to drink?" Luc closed his eyes, but didn't respond.

After a minute, he spoke in a whispered voice, "I'll be seeing mother soon. Take care of father."

"No, no, no, you can't," I sobbed. "Not now. We'll go home. You'll get better." I pressed my face to his hand and let the tears fall.

I felt a blanket being put around me, and a strong hand patted me on my shoulder. A feeling of calm came over me. My tears stopped. My mind began to wander back to when we were younger and the summer days when we played in the creek, throwing rocks and catching fish. Then I thought about Christmas when mother was still alive and father was healthy and how we sat in front of the fire and listened to him read while mother sewed. I remembered the hay fights Luc and I had in the wagon filled with freshly mowed hay as it made its way from the field to the barn.

I sat up and looked at Luc. His eyes were closed and his face wore the same expression of peace I now felt. Sergeant LaGrand pulled the sheet up over Luc's head. He helped me up and we walked downstairs into the basement kitchen. Sophie was there wiping her tears with her apron.

LaGrand sat me down at the table and said, "I'm sorry, Henri." Sophie placed a mug of hot cider in front of me and stood there, letting out an occasional burst of sobbing. I couldn't cry anymore. I knew we were in a bad spot. We would have to leave Moscow at some point and face more hardships on the way back. Perhaps it was best that Luc would not have to suffer anymore.

Jean, Serge, Phillipe, Marc, and Stosh filed in and offered their condolences. I had been on my feet every waking moment since we arrived in the city. I laid my head down on the table and slept.

When I awoke, I was lying on a mattress under a quilt near the fireplace. It looked like daylight outside from what I could see through the small windows high on the basement wall. Then the shock of Luc's death came flooding back to me.

I was alone. I sat up and pulled the quilt around me. I sat for a long time, looking at the fire. After awhile, Sophie came down the stairs.

"Where is everyone?" I asked.

"Sergeant LaGrand went to make arrangements," Sophie sobbed. "The others are out guarding the streets."

"I suppose I should go take my turn," I said as I looked around, trying to remember where I had left my musket and equipment.

"They're in the front hall," Sophie said.

I thanked her and trudged up the steps, trying to keep my mind in order, but the grief was overwhelming. I sat down on the steps and cried. Sophie joined me, and we let the tears flow. I heard footsteps come to the top of the stairs, hesitate and then leave.

After a while, the footsteps came back, and I heard Sergeant LaGrand clear his throat. He softly said, "It's time." The members of the platoon were in formation out in the street and there was a horse-drawn wagon that held Luc's body enshrouded in a sheet. I looked away.

The cemetery was just outside the city wall. A line of wagons and detachments of soldiers, just like ours, waited their turn. There was only one priest to do the funeral services. We waited in silence with bowed heads. I don't remember anything about the service.

As our procession returned to the city, it began to rain.

Chapter 32 - Occupation

Back at the house, we had our first free time in days as another unit had taken over guard duty while we were at Luc's funeral. There were about twenty of us living there, and most of the men used the time to get some sleep. Sergeant LaGrand had assigned me to a room with Jean, Serge and Stosh. It was more like a closet so we barely all fit. I didn't feel like sleeping and instead spent my time with Sophie in the kitchen. I felt less alone with her than with the men.

Luc's funeral was not the last for our platoon. We returned to the cemetery three more times over the next few days. I learned that Luc had died of typhus, and the others in the infirmary room had the same strange symptoms before they died. We didn't know for sure how the disease spread but we let the infirmary room stand empty after that.

The fires had been put out by the rain or had burned themselves out, and we only had to patrol the streets every few days. Rumor was that some units had ceased to exist. Their men had scattered and were off looting, drinking and carousing. Our platoon was able to stay together because we were all in one house, and Sergeant LaGrand kept a close watch over us. A full platoon would normally have been larger and commanded by a lieutenant, but after the battle of Borodino, there weren't enough men or officers to go around.

On most afternoons, there was a street bazaar set up by some of the soldiers and merchants as well as the peasants who were starting to come in from the countryside. There, we could buy or trade for almost anything from food to furniture to paintings to jewelry. Most of it had been looted before the fire, and very little of it was of use to a soldier in the field. That didn't stop the brisk trade.

Sometimes, I walked around the bazaar for something to do. Then, I had an idea. After months of campaigning, I felt sure the men would be eager to have their uniforms mended or new clothes made. To get started, I went back to the tailor shop. The tailor had returned, so I bought some cloth and set to work making shirts. I reasoned that having a nice, clean shirt would make a man feel good even if the rest of his clothes were falling apart. I sat down at the kitchen table and took orders from our own men and soon was on my way back to the tailor shop for more cloth and thread.

In the meantime, Sergeant LaGrand had pulled out the cloth we picked up on the first day and asked me to make greatcoats for as many of the men as possible. These long, hooded coats had sleeves wide enough that you could put one arm inside the sleeve of the other for warmth. The thick, dark blue wool would work just fine for this purpose. "Whether we're staying here all winter or not, we can use some warm coats," he said.

The tailor became curious as to what I was doing. Since neither of us spoke the other's language, I took Sophie along one day to interpret. The tailor wasn't too happy to hear he had competition. He knew somebody buying as much cloth as I was must have been up to something, but he couldn't imagine that a boy my age was doing the sewing himself. I was getting more work than I could handle so I offered to bring him in on the deal.

Each time I went to the bazaar with a sample shirt, I got enough orders to keep me busy for a few days. When I returned to the bazaar to deliver the finished shirts, I took more orders. As October came, I thought I could expand my operation and start selling greatcoats too. But I was wrong. The weather was still pleasant during the day and some men just laughed when I tried to interest them in a winter coat.

One day, Sergeant LaGrand announced that food was getting low, and we would need to go on a foraging party beyond the city walls. By now, bands of Russian cavalry and Cossacks were harassing any of our units they could find outside of the city but we had no choice. Since the Russian army itself was encamped to the south, heading north would be our best chance of finding provisions. Our haversacks contained enough food for two days when we set off.

As we left the city gates, the guards wished us luck. Even outside of the city, many of the houses were burned. They made for a dreary send-off as we left the protective walls of Moscow. Sergeant LaGrand said we should head up the main road for about five miles and then look for a road that might lead off to an estate or a village. The further away from the city we went, the more likely we would be to succeed.

We had heard many different stories from foraging parties. Some said the peasants were friendly and helpful while others told about how the villagers called in the Cossacks. We decided nobody could be trusted, and we were on our guard.

We walked the entire day. Plenty of people passed us on the main road. We knew that if there were enemy units around, we could have trouble at any time. As night fell, we headed off the road.

"We don't know if those travelers will alert the Cossacks that we're out this way so we'll get back in the woods for the night and be a little harder to find," LaGrand explained.

The next morning, we continued to travel and late in the day arrived at a village. Stosh had learned a little Russian with Sophie's help so he told the villagers that we wanted to buy a few head of cattle. They acted like they didn't know what Stosh was talking about, and he became concerned that they were trying to stall us, perhaps to give the Cossacks time to arrive.

Sergeant LaGrand soon gave up on talking to the villagers and ordered us to search the area for any food or livestock that may have been hidden away. In groups of two, we fanned out. I went with Serge. We walked between some houses and out into the woods. In a small clearing, we found some cows tied to a tree. "Well, look at this," Serge said.

As he was speaking, we heard the sound of horses crashing through the woods and a band of Cossacks bore down on us. We both raised our muskets and fired, but they kept coming. Knowing we would need to re-load, one Cossack headed straight for Serge with his sword held high. Serge reached under his coat and pulled out a pistol. The Cossack hadn't expected this and tried to turn his horse away, but it was too late. Serge fired and the startled Cossack fell to the ground as his horse raced off.

Not wanting to risk a similar fate, the remaining Cossacks turned and fled. The rest of our platoon soon arrived, alerted to our plight by the shots.

In addition to the Cossack Serge had shot with his pistol, another body was found. In the heat of the moment, I had fired at the charging men without thinking. Now one of them was dead. It may have been me who had killed him. I felt sick.

Seeing my look, Serge observed that there were two bullet holes and perhaps his shot had been the fatal one.

"But one's to the head and the other's to the chest. Either one could have ki..." I heard Marc start to say before an elbow to the ribs stopped him short.

"Alright, alright," LaGrand said, "Let's take these cows and get moving. We can't stay here and talk about it all day."

Our party arrived at the gates of Moscow two days later with six cows. We were met by the quartermaster who confiscated them all. He told us he would smoke the beef, and we could come back in a few days for our share.

Chapter 33 - The Past Returns - Again

As Sophie and I walked to the tailor shop the next day, we talked about what I needed to fill my sewing orders. Foraging had put me behind. When we got to the shop, the door was open. That was unusual, Alexi Midorovich, the tailor, always kept his door closed, even on the hottest days. He thought that a shop with a door standing open was a sign of disorder.

Sophie and I looked at each other and approached the doorway with caution. We stopped when we heard angry voices inside. I motioned for Sophie to wait while I stepped inside. The shop had been ransacked. A group of men had Mr. Midorovich surrounded, and one of them was growling at him in French.

"Where's the money old man?" said the Frenchman, his voice rising. Receiving no answer, he cuffed Mr. Midorovich on the side of the head with his hand.

I was torn between running for help and trying to stop the attack. Before I could turn and run, one of the attackers spotted me. "We have a visitor," he said while seizing my arm.

"Go for help!" I shouted out the door to Sophie as I was pulled further into the shop. The man threatening Mr. Midorovich turned to look at me. "Gaston!" I gasped.

"Well look who it is. The bread delivery boy. You filthy little runt," Gaston sneered as he recognized me. "It's about time I got even with you for turning me in to Major Pagnol. I don't see your stupid brother here so it looks like there's nobody to protect you this time. It's just you, me, and my friends."

I knew I needed to stall long enough for Sophie to get help so I started to protest that I hadn't turned him in for the bread cart incident. Then a man came through the door holding Sophie by the wrist. Sophie was whimpering and struggling as the man threw her to the floor and closed the door.

Looking at Sophie, Gaston laughed. "Ah, you do have a friend. That will make things a little more fair."

"You're nothing but a bully," I shouted at Gaston, "Leave us alone!"

"Oh, I'll leave you alone all right. Once I've kicked the snot out of you," he said taking a step toward me. I shrank back until I was next to Sophie. "There's nobody here to help you. Who's going to care about some kid and a woman? Everyone's more interested in finding another house to loot."

Gaston nodded at two of his accomplices, and one of them stepped behind me and took my arms while the other lifted Sophie up off the floor.

"Let her go!" I shouted at Gaston, "She has nothing to do with this."

"If she's a friend of yours, she needs to learn the lesson too. You both need to know how to keep your mouths shut and not go around blabbing about what happens to you."

Leaning in until we were nose-to-nose, he said, "It's your fault I spent two stinking weeks in that stockade. You and your nanny here are gonna pay."

He straightened up and then suddenly punched me in the stomach. I gasped for breath. "Whaddya have to say now, runt?" he laughed.

"That was a funny sound you just made. I wonder what sound your nanny will make," he said as he stepped in front of Sophie and delivered a blow to her stomach. Sophie gasped as she bent forward, her eyes bulging and mouth open.

I kicked and struggled against the one holding me. "You dirty bully!" I yelled, "Leave her alone!"

Stepping back in front of me, Gaston punched me again.

Mr. Midorovich huddled in the corner with his hands over his mouth and a look of terror in his eyes. I don't remember much after that. Gaston punched me a few more times in the stomach and then directed his attention to my face. I remember hearing Sophie's cries as he hit her too. When Gaston was done, I was dropped to the floor where I curled up, unable to move. Someone gave me a kick, then the door closed, and all was quiet.

I tried to sit up, but my ribs hurt too much. I looked up at Mr. Midorovich, "Go," I gasped, waving my hand at the door. Even though he didn't speak French, he understood what I was asking him to do. I knew Sophie had told him where we lived, and I hoped he knew how to get there. Sophie and I lay on the floor for what seemed like an hour whispering words of encouragement to each other.

Finally, the door burst open, and I could hear the voices of Serge and Stosh. "Who did this?" Serge was shouting, "I will kill them! Do you hear me? I will kill them!"

Stosh was trying to calm him down, "There will be plenty of time for killing later. For now, we need to get these two back to the house. C'mon, you're bigger, you carry Sophie."

Stosh hoisted me up. Being carried did not help my ribs or my pride. Soon, I was lying on a bed with a wet cloth on my face. My eyes were both swelling, and it was hard to see. I could hear a lot of commotion, though, and most of it was hurried and angry.

Sergeant LaGrand leaned over me, "Who did this to you?" he asked in a soothing voice.

"Is Sophie going to be all right?" I asked.

"She'll be fine. Just tell me who it was," LaGrand persisted.

"It was Gaston Brasheer," I said with some difficulty.

"Who's he? What regiment is he with?"

I had taken note of Gaston's uniform while he was threatening me. "The 30th," I answered.

"They're with Davout's corps. The dirty buggers," LaGrand muttered. "Now tell me, what did he look like?"

"You know him, Sergeant," I whispered, "He was in our recruiting party. He was the big red-haired bully."

"That son-of-a..., I should have guessed," LaGrand muttered. "You stay here and rest up," he said patting my leg.

"Where are you going?" I asked as he left the room, but he didn't answer. I heard loud clattering and lots of footsteps in the hallway as muskets and equipment bumped and rattled. Then the men were filing out the door.

Out on the street I heard Captain Blanc's voice and then LaGrand's. Captain Blanc came into my room and stood over me taking in my bruised and battered face. He turned away without saying anything and spoke to LaGrand and the men who had returned to the hallway. "I see our man has taken a beating, and I know why you are eager for revenge." There were murmurs of agreement in the hall. "However, I can't allow you to take up arms against another French unit."

LaGrand exploded in protest, "But you see what he's done. He has it coming!" I had never heard LaGrand so angry.

"You and I both know it, but I doubt his comrades or commanding officer will see it that way. Now stand down and put away your guns. I will file a protest with Marshal Davout's headquarters."

At the mention of a "protest" the men burst out with angry talk. Someone said, "I'll file my protest with a musket ball."

"Gentlemen!" Captain Blanc snapped. "Like it or not, we are in the army. If we start fighting each other, none of us will ever get back to France. Now lay down your weapons, and let me handle this." As the Captain strode out of the room, I could hear him tell Sergeant LaGrand, "I'm holding you responsible for their actions."

Chapter 34 - Preparing to Leave

After the grumbling stopped, I drifted off into sleep. I don't know how long I slept, but when I woke up, Sophie was sitting in a chair next to my bed. Her face was bruised, and one of her eyes was swollen shut, but she smiled at me. It was good to see her up and moving. I was surprised to see Mr. Midorovich was also in the room. Sophie told me he had not left the house for fear of the bullies returning. He wasn't sitting idle, though. He had found my pile of cloth and unfilled orders and had been sewing shirts and coats while watching over Sophie and me.

Marc had been appointed cook while Sophie recovered, and he came into the room with a thin soup. "I'd tell you I made it thin on account of your sore face, but the fact is, we don't have much left to put in the soup," Marc explained. Marc had a gift for speaking his mind regardless of the situation.

I thanked him and asked if there was any news I missed. "Well, we'll be leaving the city soon and heading west for winter quarters. Let's see, what else? Oh, our corps is going to parade for the Emperor in a few days. I think you heard the part about how we aren't allowed to kill Gaston."

I thanked him and, with great effort, sat up. Sophie tried to get me to lie down again, but I told her if the army was leaving, I was going under my own power. With her help, I stood up and stiffly walked around the room before collapsing back on the bed. I suggested she leave me and start packing for the march. She looked away.

"What's the matter? You are coming with us. Aren't you?" I asked, now worried.

Sophie shook her head and choked back tears. "But you can't stay here," I protested.

"I don't have anywhere to go," she replied in a soft voice. "When the army is gone, the masters will return and everything will be back the way it was."

"Won't they be mad at you for helping us? We're the enemy."

Sophie shrugged, "I don't know if they'll be mad or not, but my job was to stay at the house and watch over it. That's what I've done."

Changing the subject, she continued, "Sergeant LaGrand has given the men assignments of things to gather and pack. He said once the army is outside of the city, you'll all be on your own."

Looking down at the floor, she spied my shoes. "He wants everyone to have a good pair of shoes. I think yours could use a few repairs," she said as she held them up. One of the soles flapped. Seeing this, Mr. Midorovich took the shoes and walked out. Sophie and I looked at each other as we heard the door close.

Later that evening, Mr. Midorovich returned. He held my shoes up so I could see they had been repaired and polished. They looked as good as the day I first put them on. I smiled and looked as Sophie. After a brief exchange, Sophie explained that the tailor knew a cobbler who owed him a favor. The cobbler had protested about repairing a stinking Frenchman's shoes. Midorovich told him to hold his nose and get to work.

Mr. Midorovich pulled a pair of long, thick socks out from a sack he was holding. He handed them to me with tears in his eyes and left the room. "He's very grateful for what you've done for him." Sophie said, "Giving him business and treating him fairly."

"I'll thank him when he comes back," I said.

"He's not coming back. He thinks the evacuation will bring on more looting and destruction."

By the next day I was out of bed. I pronounced myself well and reported to Sergeant LaGrand for orders. He took note of my refurbished shoes, and said I had to gather everything else I needed to survive a winter campaign.

"Deliver the rest of your sewing goods to the marketplace, but don't take any more orders. Buy up anything you think will be of use such as socks, mittens, knit hats, dried foods if you can find them, candles, spare musket parts, pocket knives, lanterns, blankets, salt, tobacco, things like that."

The bazaar was busier than ever on that day. When word reached the surrounding countryside that the army was leaving, peasants flocked to the city from miles around to sell as much as they could before the army left. There was not much of use; however, I was able to get some salt, a few candles and musket flints.

As I left the bazaar, happy with my practical purchases, something caught my eye. It was a silver necklace with a small, intricate cross. I wanted to buy it as a gift for Sophie. By now, I had learned how to bargain. I asked the man how much, as if I were mildly curious. When I heard the price, I apologized and started to walk away. The man called after me, "I can make a deal."

I turned back and asked what kind of deal. "A special deal, just for you. The army is leaving soon, and I would rather carry the money than all of this merchandise," he said gesturing to the blanket covered with goods. His next price wasn't much better. I shrugged my shoulders, said, "Thanks anyway," and started to leave.

"No, no, no," the man said running after me and putting his arm around my shoulder to guide me back. "I can see you are a discriminating buyer, what will it take for you and this beautiful necklace to be together?"

I fished in my haversack and pulled out one gold coin. "I'll give you this coin for it if you throw in that book," I said pointing at a volume on the history of Russia on the corner of the blanket. It had been written by a Frenchman.

"Ah, you wound me," the man said clutching his heart with both hands.

I was in the middle of saying, "Sorry it didn't work out," when the man snatched the coin, handed me the necklace, pointed at the book, and said, "Take it."

I scooped up the book and hurried off. Back at the house, LaGrand and the men were muttering about something. "What's wrong?" I asked.

"When we went to get our beef from the quartermaster, he said it had already been given away," growled Marc who, as cook, seemed to take it especially hard. It sounded like something the army would do - let us risk our lives to bring back the cattle and then give it away to somebody else.

"Pack inspection in one hour," LaGrand bellowed up the stairs. "Parade inspection one hour after that."

I went to my room and spread out my things on the mattress. Taking careful inventory, I packed all of my belongings. From Luc's pack, I pulled a plug of tobacco, a journal with sporadic entries and some letters from Cressida tied with a red ribbon.

With some squeezing and re-arranging, everything fit. Then, I unpacked each item and laid it back on my mattress so Sergeant LaGrand could inspect. While I was waiting for the inspection, Serge handed me a pistol.

"Where did you get it?" I asked.

"Someone, ah, gave it to me, and I already have one," Serge said as he threw a small pouch with some lead balls and a few cartridges on to my pile.

"Thank you!" I exclaimed. Stosh and Jean looked on, smiling.

Sergeant LaGrand made the rounds, examining the contents of each man's pack. He was not pleased I had packed my recently acquired book. "You will probably toss it aside before long," he concluded.

One hour later, LaGrand assembled us on the street for parade inspection. He was less concerned about how we looked than how well equipped we were. He spent a great deal of time examining the contents of our cartridge boxes, making sure there were plenty of rounds and spare flints.

After inspection, we filed back inside for a supper Sophie had prepared. She had pulled a ham and potatoes from somewhere and prepared a feast to go along with the freshly baked bread. During the meal, Sergeant LaGrand told us we were to have a review in front of Napoleon the next morning and then leave the city the following day.

We talked and laughed and tried not to think about our impending departure. We were glad to be heading toward home, yet apprehensive about what we would face. The march in had been hard enough, but now supplies were low again, and the army was not in very good shape. The worst parts for me, though, were leaving Sophie behind and knowing that Luc would not be with me.

Chapter 35 - The Retreat Begins

The next morning, we formed in the street just as the sun was coming over the tops of the houses. As usual, when various units need to meet and march, there was a lot of waiting. By the time all units were in place, it was almost noon.

The Kremlin is a walled city in itself, and it had escaped the fire. We marched in and straight toward a large open square where the most beautiful church I had ever seen rose up in front of us. Men near me said it was St. Basil's church. It had numerous onion shaped domes, each a different color, and they sparkled in the midday sun. I was so captivated by the sight of those domes, that I once again missed catching a glimpse of Napoleon as we passed through the square.

We continued past St. Basil's and out a gate at the opposite end of the Kremlin wall. We kept marching until we were back in front of our house. Once dismissed, we put the house back in order and loaded up a horse drawn cart some of the men had procured. We didn't have much in the way of food to load. The remainder of the space was taken up with furniture, women's gowns, candle sticks and even a box of china. LaGrand rolled his eyes when he saw that but didn't say anything.

In the morning, we re-packed our personal gear and prepared to leave. It was with a heavy heart that I went down into the kitchen to bid Sophie farewell. I told her I would miss her and never forget her or all of the kind things she had done for Luc and me. As I said this, I handed her the silver necklace from the bazaar. She looked at it for a long moment and her eyes welled up with tears. She kissed the cross and handed it back to me. "Thank you, Henri, but I cannot keep this. I want you to take it home with you to France and give it the girl who captures your heart. Someday you can tell your grandchildren about me." As she pressed the necklace into my hand, I heard the call to assemble in the street. I gave Sophie a hug and hurried up the stairs.

As we stood in formation, I looked around the street, trying to remember each detail. I thought about how I would be leaving Luc's grave behind. I consoled myself with the fact that I had his journal and the other mementos I would be taking home where they belonged.

The order came to march, and we made our way through the city and out the gate. Rather than head due west along the route we had come in, we were taking a southwestern route. This way, we would travel through countryside that hadn't already been ravaged by our army for food and supplies.

The weather was beautiful and warm. Looking around, I could see carts, carriages and wagons of every description loaded with plunder. Soldiers were carrying bundles under their arms, in bags strapped across their shoulders, or even on litters between two men. There were a good number of women and even children in the column as well. I had heard many French citizens had been living in Moscow. When they chose to stay in the city after our occupation, their lot had been cast. They feared the consequences if they stayed behind. All in all, our column had the look of a travelling carnival.

The journey on that first day did not seem so bad, but by evening, we began to pass things that had been discarded by the soldiers. It was possible to pick up items that had been purchased in the bazaar just the day before. The only price to pay now was the labor to carry it all the way back to France.

With so much baggage, the army moved slower than it had on the way in to Moscow. The horses pulling the wagons and carriages were in a weaker condition and soon some of them broke down and could go no further. More than once we passed a wagon loaded with treasures and the driver cursing at his horse who had collapsed in the harness.

As he had on the way in, Sergeant LaGrand worked to keep our platoon together. The men who had the horse and cart often fell behind, and at first LaGrand had us wait for them to catch up, but after awhile, he abandoned this plan. Our provisions were removed from the cart and distributed among the rest of the platoon to carry. We never saw the men or their cart again.

On the morning of the third day, the rain began. The road turned to mud, and the vehicles sank in and became stuck. Men fell and struggled back to their feet soaked and muddy. It rained too hard to make a fire for the night so we huddled under a tree. We still had some of the food we had started with, but the prospects of getting more were looking bad so we began to ration it, remembering the hunger from the march in.

A few days later, the column came to a stop as we heard the sound of cannons and musket fire up ahead. This exchange went on for hours. Smoke could be seen in the distance as night fell and the sounds of battle came to an end.

In the morning, word came down through the column to move off to the side of the road. The column was turning around. As the Italian regiments from the front marched by, we could see they had been in a terrible fight. They told us there had been a fierce battle with the Russian army at a town called Maloyaroslavets. It was burned to the ground with much loss of life. Since our path had been blocked, we had to re-trace our steps. The weather was good. We had hopes there would be a late winter as we headed back to the road that would take us north to Borodino.

Three days after we had turned north, we saw buzzards circling in the air ahead. We were approaching the Borodino battlefield. Nothing could prepare us for what we saw there. It had been almost two months since the battle, but the battlefield looked untouched. Dead horses and men were strewn everywhere in various stages of decay. The smell was horrible. Buzzards and crows perched on the bodies as our column streamed by. We passed along behind the flèche we had captured. The cannon I had manned was still there, pointing in the same direction I had left it.

The sight of the battlefield was gruesome and demoralizing, but it was nothing compared to what we were about to see. The column continued to the Moscow-Smolensk road that ran through the town of Borodino. A number of the buildings had been converted into hospitals, and they were still filled with men who had been too badly wounded to be transported into Moscow. When the wounded saw the army passing by, they dragged themselves outside begging to be taken along. To be left behind meant death at the hands of the avenging Russians.

These doomed men saw the carts, wagons and carriages rolling by loaded with plunder. When it became clear that the drivers were too greedy to make room for the wounded, some of the injured men shouted and cursed, while others asked to be shot. They could not understand how their fellow soldiers could leave them to face certain death while carrying furniture, tapestries, paintings and fine dresses back to France.

As our platoon passed through the village, LaGrand ordered us to keep our eyes to the front. It wasn't necessary. None of us had any desire to look the condemned men in the eye.

During this time, the Russian army itself did not bother us. We only saw Cossacks and strange horsemen, called Bashkirs, who rode on small, ugly horses and fired arrows at us from a distance. We could laugh at them, for now.

Stories began to reach us about the fate that would befall a single soldier or small unit caught by Russian peasants away from the main column. The stories were very detailed about the kind of revenge the Russians would take. They always ended with the death of the unfortunate captives. As a result, we didn't dare venture far from the road unless in a large group.

Chapter 36 - A Change of Position

The last days of October passed. As part of Ney's Third Corps, we were in the middle of the column with Davout's First Corps bringing up the rear as we headed toward Viasma. Travelling in a column meant the first units passed over the road when it was in good shape, but the ones that followed had to pass through the debris and ruts from the lead units. This slowed the rest of the column and caused gaps.

The baggage train for our corps began to fall behind leaving long stretches without any soldiers to protect it. The Cossacks took advantage of this situation not far out of Viasma. They swooped down on the helpless wagons and made off with horses and supplies. Davout's rearguard corps were temporarily cut off, causing a panic among them.

Our Corps had made it into Viasma when word of the attack arrived. Ney ordered all units to assemble and head back out to cover the approach of the rest of the column. We stood guard along the road as what was left of the baggage train straggled in.

Toward dusk, the first elements of the rearguard began to arrive, but close behind them came the regular Russian army. When the Russians opened fire, Davout's corps, frightened earlier by the Cossack raid, broke and ran toward Viasma. Ney's corps returned fire with the Russians while the First Corps jammed the entrance to the town. Fortunately, the Russians were in no mood for a fight and soon retired, but it was the behavior of our fellow Frenchmen that had the veterans of our regiment talking. They had never witnessed such panic in French troops before and saw it as a bad omen.

The speed with which the panic in the First Corps had spread was frightening. I thought back to the words of my father about how the line between victory and defeat could be thin. The panic of a few had almost brought disaster.

As night fell, so did the first snow of the winter. The temperature dropped, and we put on our greatcoats for the first time as we stood watch outside the town. We grumbled that Davout's men were enjoying the pleasures and safety of the town while we stood out in the snow, keeping watch.

After the disaster at Viasma, Napoleon issued orders that Ney's corps was to assume the rearguard position and keep the Russian army from following too close. In addition, the baggage train was ordered to travel in the middle of the column, flanked by troops on either side to protect it from the Cossacks.

It was now much colder than it had been even the day before. I tried to find ways to keep my mind from thinking about how numb my fingers and toes were and how I hadn't eaten in more than a day.

Once the lead units had passed over the road, the snow became packed and slippery. Men and horses had trouble keeping their footing. As we approached one of the larger hills, discarded plunder lined either side of the road. Men had given up on carrying their fortune home and were now just trying to survive.

As bad as things became for the men, they were worse for the horses who could not find any forage, yet were pulling overloaded wagons along icy roads. Men were drafted from the column to help push carriages and wagons up some of the hills, a task nobody wished to perform - especially when it was a fancy carriage carrying an officer and his mistress.

There was no relief from the cold. The need to stay close to the road for safety from the Cossacks and peasants made foraging for firewood difficult. We were often kept busy responding to the cry of "Cossacks!" as panicked troops jumped at every shadow.

It was on the second night after we left Viasma that I too, parted with a piece of my "plunder." The column had stopped for the night, and we were struggling to light fires for warmth. In this particular spot, we had enough firewood, but nothing to get the fire going. I reached into my pack and pulled out *The History of Russia*. I turned to the back where there were a few blank pages, tore them out and handed them to Serge who had been trying to start the fire with twigs and moss.

"No bedtime story tonight, eh?" he said as he took the pages.

I still held out hope I could one day read the book, but without a fire, none of us would live to read anything. Stosh had been holding onto a piece of dried beef, and he cut it up and passed it around. "Enjoy it," he said, "it's all I have left."

In the morning, Phillipe did not move. The fire had gone out, and he had frozen where he lay. Sergeant LaGrand was angry at himself for not insisting we wake up throughout the night and move around to keep from freezing.

The uniforms worn by the Grande Armée were not suited for the winter. The coats were thin and designed so they cut away in the front. We had not been issued winter pants, and those we had were worn thin from months of campaigning. Our platoon was in pretty good shape for shoes, but most of the army was nearly barefoot. The greatcoats were a savior to us and many men offered to buy or trade for them. There were also men who began to protect themselves from the cold by wearing the gowns and furs they were carrying home to wives or sweethearts.

Around this time an order was issued that all horses were to be transferred to the artillery to pull the guns. This order caused a major uproar as it meant carriages and wagons with wounded men and treasures would have to be left behind. We experienced scenes as heart-wrenching as those at Borodino had been.

Anyone too injured to walk no longer had a way to continue the journey. As we passed the abandoned wagons, the wounded men called out, asking for us to take pity and carry them with us. As before, a few of them asked to be shot, but none of us had the heart to do it. If they were fortunate, the severe cold would kill them before long. Perhaps they could fall asleep and never wake up as Phillipe had done.

A few nights out of Viasma, a blizzard hit. The wind cut through our clothes, and our feet were so numb we couldn't feel the ground we were walking on. It became difficult to stay together when darkness came and the wind and snow continued. We couldn't get a fire started so LaGrand came around every hour to make each of us stand and move around to keep from freezing.

We often saw Marshal Ney stride through the camp giving orders and encouragement. It was impossible not to catch his enthusiasm and energy when he was around. I don't know when either he or Sergeant LaGrand slept during those days.

Chapter 37 - Stragglers

After two days, the blizzard ended, and the full extent of the army's disarray was revealed. Discarded muskets stuck out of the snow, frozen bodies lay as if they were taking a nap, men and even women struggled along holding onto each other. With the exception of the rearguard, it became apparent the army no longer existed. It was now a collection of stragglers whose goal was to preserve their own lives, at the expense of their comrades if necessary.

Theft was rampant and many men formed gangs for mutual protection. Stragglers on their own were doomed. Once our rearguard passed them by, they would either freeze or be tortured to death by the peasants. We told any straggler we saw that we were the last allied unit and after us the Russians would be coming. Some of them sat down to await their fate.

It was a wonder there were any horses left. We passed their carcasses by the score. They had been shod with the wrong kind of shoes so they often slipped on the slick ground breaking a leg. The others had succumbed to the cold, the unending work, and lack of food.

Our next destination was Smolensk, the city we had left smoldering after the battle in August. The army had maintained a garrison there so we hoped to find food and shelter.

Our platoon had one heavy cooking pot. We all took turns carrying it, but somewhere along the way it was lost. Everyone pointed at Stosh, but he denied losing it. He said he had handed it off to someone, but couldn't remember who.

Most of the time we had nothing to cook anyway. One day, however, Serge came up with a little meat and what he said was a potato. He was rather evasive on where it had come from, and we didn't press him too hard. These ingredients would make a nice stew if we could find a pot to make it in. A few campfires away, some men with a pot were trying to start a fire. They had been at it for a long time without success so I approached and asked what their terms would be for lending us the pot.

"It's not for lending," one of them snapped.

"Do you need help getting your fire started?" I asked.

"No! Now leave us alone." He turned to glare up at me, but stopped when he saw me tearing pages out of my book. His eyes lit up.

"You can use it when we're done," he said.

I handed him the pages and looked at the pot. "Are those turnips?" I asked.

"Look, we already made a deal for the paper..." his voice trailed off when he saw me holding up a small container.

"Would you like some salt in your stew?" I asked.

His companions looked at each other eagerly, as I thought they might. One of their stew ingredients was tree bark. That would taste a lot better with seasoning. The man nodded.

"How many turnips worth of salt would you like?" I asked.

I walked back to our group with three turnips. Then we sat, watching the men with the pot cook their stew. It seemed to take forever. When they had served each man his portion, I ran over and grabbed the pot. We dumped in the beef, potato, turnips, some salt and water and then sat around the fire helping it boil by watching it with anticipation. In the end, we each had three mouthfuls of the stew, but it was worth it.

Later that night, it was our platoon's turn to man the picket posts. This was a boring, yet frightening job. Standing a short distance from camp, we looked for signs of the enemy.

It was a clear night with just enough wind to move the tree branches. The moon was almost full which combined with the snow made for good visibility. I was just thinking about how the cold penetrated straight to my bones when I thought I heard a person talking out in the woods. I forgot all about the cold. Who would be out there?

I took a few steps forward. There it was again. I wished the wind would stop so I could hear better. I took a few more steps and heard it again. It didn't sound like talking, but it was a human. I looked back at the campfires. Should I raise the alarm? If someone was going to attack, they wouldn't be talking so loud. I thought I would just go a little further and see what was going on.

The snow muffled my steps as I walked slowly forward, my musket at the ready. There was definitely a man talking, and I could make out some French words. I followed the sound but took care to be silent myself. I could see people up ahead.

As I crept a little closer, I could make out the scene. Three men were tied to trees and two of them were slumped over. A group of Russian peasants were gathered around the last conscious man and were taking turns beating him with a stick. After each blow, the man would moan and mutter in French. My heart began to pound in my chest. The peasants were so caught up in the beating that they hadn't seen me, but the victim raised his head a little and looked straight at me, pleading for help. I recognized him. It was Gaston. One of the peasants followed his gaze and saw me as I was turning to go get help.

Trapped, I faced them and raised my musket. With as much confidence as I could muster, I shouted, "Stop." Seeing just one soldier, and a boy at that, the attackers relaxed, and the biggest one stepped toward me chuckling with a menacing grin. It was clear he didn't think a boy would have the guts to shoot. I couldn't let him get closer. Taking careful aim at his chest, I pulled the trigger. The grin left his face, his eyes rolled up into his head, his knees buckled, and he slumped to the snow. The peasants looked at the body in surprise then looked at me with revenge in their eyes. They knew I wouldn't have time to reload, and they outnumbered me.

Three scowling men came toward me. I reached under my coat, pulled out my pistol and held it steady, pointing at the men.

By now desperation had taken over, and I had no fear. "Who's next?" I said. The men stopped as I aimed the pistol from man to man. "Cut them down," I said, gesturing to the prisoners. Nobody moved so I stepped forward, still pointing the pistol, and said forcefully, "Now!"

They didn't speak French, but the pistol told them all they needed to know. The prisoners were cut down, and they dropped into the snow. "Now go," I said, waving the pistol. The group slowly backed away and then broke into a run when they saw soldiers coming up behind me.

Serge and Stosh stopped on either side of me and watched the peasants hurrying off. "What happened? Who are those men?" Serge asked.

"They're French. Those peasants were beating them to death," I said as we knelt by the men.

"This one is dead," Stosh said.

"Let's get the other two back to camp," Serge sighed, slipping his arm under the now unconscious Gaston and hoisting him across his shoulders.

Once we had lain them by our fire, Serge looked down at them. "I wonder who they are?"

"I don't know who that one is," I said pointing, "but this one is Gaston."

They looked at me in shock. Marc was the first to recover by saying, "Should we shoot him now or wake him up first?"

Stosh exclaimed, "Are you saying that out of the thousands of men in this army, you risked your life to save the one that nearly killed you and Sophie?"

Sergeant LaGrand just shook his head and muttered, "Well, don't that beat all."

It was hard for me to feel angry at Gaston after seeing the way he had suffered. The peasants must have extracted their revenge on the men one at a time until they thought they were dead. I had interrupted them when they were working over Gaston.

The next morning, Gaston regained consciousness, but his companion did not. Gaston was lucky in one way. Because his legs were uninjured, he was able to walk. A shirt and coat were found for him, and he hobbled along with the rest of the stragglers when the column resumed the march. Before he headed off, he looked at me as if he were about to say something, but instead, lowered his eyes and walked away.

Chapter 38 - The Return to Smolensk

We approached Smolensk late in the day, dreaming of the food and shelter we might find there, but knowing as last in the column, our chances of getting any of it were poor. Upon entering the city, we were met with a scene of chaos. Groups of soldiers milled about, some were fighting each other. Campfires were burning here and there in the street. Parts of buildings were being torn down for firewood causing those who were seeking shelter in them to protest. In the half-light, it was an eerie and frightening sight.

Sergeant LaGrand kept us together as we made our way through the city to where we hoped the quartermaster would be distributing provisions. When we arrived at the building there was a crowd of men around the door, shouting and pushing. An officer was standing in the doorway, but it was hard to hear what he was saying over the noise. At last, the officer gave up, stepped aside, and the crowd surged in.

LaGrand told us to wait while he went and talked to the officer. Then they both came over to where our platoon waited. I didn't recognize the officer at first as he hadn't shaved in a few days and his uniform was covered with a ragged cape made from a blanket. But when he spoke, I knew who it was.

"Captain Faber!" I exclaimed.

He looked at me with weary eyes and said, "It's Major now. Not that it matters. Nice to see you again, Henri. You're looking well."

Sergeant LaGrand spoke up, "I was just asking the good Major about provisions for the rearguard."

Major Faber looked at us and sighed, "I know you won't want to hear this after putting your lives on the line protecting this rabble that used to be an army, but the stores of food are gone. The first units to arrive broke in and took everything. We tried to explain that more men were coming, and they needed food too, but it was like trying to talk a dog out of a bone." He nodded toward the storehouse and continued, "Those men in there will come out in a minute and be angry at me for not having something for them, but it's gone now, all gone."

Sure enough, the men who had entered the storehouse reappeared looking about wildly for Major Faber. When they spotted him talking to our platoon, a thin soldier with a ragged beard and bulging eyes came running toward us pointing an accusing finger and shouting, "You vile betrayer! You sold our food! We're starving, and you sold it!"

The man was approaching so fast and was so enraged, that we instinctively readied our muskets to make him and the crowd stop. Their anger continued to boil. With only ten feet separating our platoon from the mob, the situation was tense. Major Faber tried to speak, raising his hands and asking for calm, but he was shouted down. A piece of wood came flying at us from the back of the mob.

"Hold your fire, men," LaGrand growled in a low voice as the wood sailed over our heads. A few more pieces flew and then a rock. The situation was getting worse in a hurry. I think Sergeant LaGrand was about to give the order to fire when a single figure came bursting in and stood between the two groups. It was Marshal Ney, and he was in a fury. The thin soldier with the beard began to shout at Ney who struck him across the face so hard the man staggered into the man behind him.

The mob fell silent. Marshal Ney was known to everyone in the army and was held in the highest regard. He was often in the front lines in battle and was without fear. The men respected and loved him, even those not under his command.

Ney faced the mob and spoke, "We've been out there on the road, too, and we won't be eating tonight either. Now go back to your billets. The enemy is gathering around us, and we can't be fighting among ourselves."

The mob murmured and men broke off from the edges and drifted away.

Ney turned to Major Faber, "Major, is there anything that can be found for my men?"

"I'm sorry, sir," Faber replied, "It's all been looted."

Marshal Ney didn't say a word, but stalked off. After he was gone, Major Faber told LaGrand that Napoleon had wanted to spend the remainder of the winter there, but after seeing the condition of the city, he changed his mind. "My advice to you," Faber said, "is to get out of the city and don't get caught up in this mess. I think we'll be evacuating in the next day or two."

With that, we turned and headed back outside the city. It was odd to think it was safer outside the walls than in the city with our own troops. We found a burned out house that still had three walls standing and made ourselves as comfortable as possible. As we settled down for the night, we tried to ignore our growling stomachs.

Around midnight, an officer came with orders from Colonel de Pelleport, our regimental commander. The army was to begin leaving the next day, but the Third Corps was to stay behind and blow up the city walls.

When the officer left, the grumbling began. Everyone thought it useless to destroy a city we were abandoning.

"Those are the orders," LaGrand said, "We just carry them out."

He was right, but complaining is a favorite pass-time of soldiers, and it took our minds off our hunger and numb limbs.

In the morning, we set about our task. While the food supplies were gone, there was plenty of gunpowder. We worked to stack it against the walls.

It took all day to get the charges in place. The plan was for us to spend the night and blow the walls in the morning. We were able to find a building with a roof and spent our first night indoors since leaving Moscow.

In the morning, some men were chosen to stay behind and light the fuses. As we left, we heard the pleas of the wounded who knew they would soon be at the mercy of the Russians. Some of them had been there since the battle in August; others had struggled there from further east but could go no further. Sergeant LaGrand once again reminded us to look straight ahead; if we made eye contact with them the vision would haunt us forever.

We stopped on a hill to watch the destruction. The last time I had been on that hill, it had been August, and I was still a teamster. Below, I could see the stream where I had filled the canteens and exchanged gifts with the Russians. Uppermost in my mind was that the last time I had stood there, Luc had been alive.

Dull thuds from down in the city snapped me back to the present. Puffs of smoke came up from the far side of the city. There were more explosions and smoke as the charges were set off in order, working their way around the wall. After a few minutes the men who had set off the explosions came out of the city and climbed the hill to join us. We all stood together watching. Our charges seemed to do little damage, but no one suggested going back to try again.

Chapter 39 - LaGrand's Order

We turned our backs on Smolensk and worked on catching up to the main column. It was still our job to protect the rear of the retreating army. We pressed on for hours, urging the stragglers from the forward units on ahead of us. In the early afternoon, our march gained more urgency as we heard the sound of cannons and muskets up ahead. As we got closer, the sounds died away.

From a distance, we could see a line of soldiers with cannons blocking the road. The Russian army had cut us off. Word filtered back that the Russians had approached Marshal Ney under a flag of truce claiming he was surrounded and offering to let him surrender. To our joy, Ney had refused, saying that a Marshal of France never surrenders.

Orders were given for us to form up and fix bayonets. We were going to push our way through. "Check your weapons and ammunition, lads," Sergeant LaGrand ordered. "We'll need all the firepower we can get."

Drawn up in battle formation, it was easy to see how depleted the ranks were. Behind us, I could see there were twice as many stragglers as armed soldiers. Among them were old men, women and a few children. We were their only hope.

The Russian artillery opened fire, and we began moving forward as shots fell around us. We kept advancing until we were well within range of the Russian line, then stopped and fired a volley before advancing some more. We were at very close range pouring volley after volley into their line, but the Russians still held.

When we were within 30 paces, the order to "charge bayonets" was given. We dropped our muskets from our shoulders to the charge position as we shouted "Huzzah!" Then came the order to "Charge!" and our line broke into a run as we all let out a yell. We crashed into the enemy line, and our two sides slugged it out until we were ordered to withdraw. Their ranks had stood firm.

We withdrew to the place where we had opened the battle. Many of our men could be seen lying on the ground in front of the Russian line. Troops were shifted to fill out the ranks in various units. I looked around our platoon, but couldn't find Marc or Jean. Serge said he saw Marc go down after getting hit in the leg. Nobody was sure where Jean was.

Sergeant LaGrand told us to wipe our muskets down and re-fill our cartridge boxes. We followed the same tactics as before, marching across the open, snow-covered field and firing at close range before closing with the bayonets. The results were the same, and our line began to fall back in ragged formation, firing and reloading as we withdrew. As we retreated, I could see that our regimental flag had been captured. The Russians were celebrating by waving it over their heads.

I had become separated from my platoon. Dusk was approaching, and I quickly became desperate. With everyone wearing coats, blankets and capes over their uniforms, it wasn't possible to tell which regiment anyone was with. I ran through the disorganized units, becoming more and more frantic. I was in tears when Serge found me. He took a firm grip on my arm and led me to a huddled group.

I saw Stosh and Sergeant LaGrand. LaGrand was wounded in the leg, but he lay there calmly. I knelt by him and grabbed the front of his coat. "We're going to get out of this," I cried, "tell me we'll make it out."

"Now, now, Henri," he said in a soothing voice, "we're not done yet. It'll take a lot more soldiers than the Russians have to stop 'ole Ney. Now go gather up some firewood. We're going to be here for the night."

I looked at Stosh who nodded. "We've been ordered to build fires. We'll need enough wood to keep them going all night."

He got up and took my shoulder and led me to the woods. We each returned with an armload of wood. I pulled out my copy of *The History of Russia* and tore out some more pages. We soon had a blazing fire going, and I could look around and see that other fires were lit throughout our camp. The light was fading when Serge came back, supporting Marc. I gasped in horror. Marc's leg was missing below the knee. Serge laid him down near the fire.

Marc buried his face in his hands. Then he shook his head, looked up at Serge, and said, "Do you think you could go back and find my other shoe?" We all chuckled a little but knew the fate of someone who could not walk.

Sergeant LaGrand sat up and told me I should head out to the battlefield now that the shooting had stopped and gather up cartridges because we were running very low. Even though Stosh was also uninjured, I was to go by myself. I was given a few cartridges out of Marc's box, just in case, and sent out into the gathering darkness. I picked my way through the battle aftermath and gathered up as many cartridges as I could carry.

Back at the fire, I gave cartridges to Serge, Stosh and myself. I went to put some in Sergeant LaGrand's cartridge box, but he stayed my hand and said, "Henri, I need to talk to you." I knelt by his side, and he said, "The army is going to slip away tonight. You can't make it through the Russians in front of us so you are going to have to go around by heading back toward Smolensk and then north to cross the Dnieper River."

"Don't you mean, 'we'?" I asked.

"The fires are going to be left burning so the Russians won't know you're gone," he said ignoring my question. "Someone needs to keep them going."

"No!" I interrupted, "you'll be coming with us."

"I can't walk, but I can drag myself from fire to fire," he explained.

"We'll carry you," I said with tears filling my eyes. "We need you," I pleaded.

"You know it's impossible for a man to make it through these conditions without two healthy legs. I can at least do this one last thing for my platoon. I've had enough adventures in this army for two life-times. This will be the last and greatest one. Now listen, this is an order. I want you, Serge and Stosh to stay alive. You stick together and do whatever you have to do, but you get home alive. Do you understand that order?" he said firmly.

I nodded, and he continued. "Now say goodbye to Marc and gather your things, you'll be leaving soon." I stood up, holding back tears and walked over to Marc.

Marc was very pale and hadn't moved in a long time, but he looked up at me and held out his fist. "Open your hand," he said. I did so and he dropped a few cartridges into it. "These belong to the Russians, and I need you to go give them back," he closed his eyes.

"I will," I said, a bit confused.

He looked up again and said, "Right between the eyes."

Chapter 40 - The Night March

We walked behind the burning fires so our shadows could not be seen from the Russian side and slipped back down the road toward Smolensk. Word was passed that silence was of the utmost importance. The burning fires would hold the Russian's attention only if we were quiet. I took one last look back at the campfires and said a silent goodbye to Sergeant LaGrand and Marc.

Serge, Stosh, and I walked along and soon found ourselves near the head of the corps where Marshal Ney was leading the column. I could hear him consulting with his officers from time to time about which way to go and whether to wait for everyone to catch up. The decision was always to keep going. The stragglers could catch up, but the lead element had to find the way as fast as possible.

The night was very dark. This turned out to be good and bad. On the good side, it kept us from being seen by the Russians as we made our escape. On the bad side, it made it hard to keep everyone together and see where we were going

After a few hours, Ney became concerned about where we were. I could hear him repeating, "We should have been there by now." Serge said he must be referring to the Dnieper River that lay to our north. We came upon a gully with a small, frozen stream at the bottom. Everyone stopped while Ney pondered what to do. After a minute, he turned to me and said, "Go down and break a hole in that ice and see which way the stream is flowing."

I suppose he picked me because I looked nimble enough to get up and down the snow-covered sides of the gully. I broke open a hole in the ice with the butt of my musket, but couldn't see well enough to determine the direction of the water flow. Looking around, I found a twig and dropped it through the hole. I watched it get washed under the ice and pointed in the direction the twig had gone.

An hour later, we emerged from the trees at the bank of the river. Ney turned to me again and asked me to walk out onto the ice to test the strength. Serge and Stosh both volunteered to go with me, but Ney said he wanted the lightest first.

I moved out from the bank, sliding my feet along. After the cold we had experienced, I was sure the ice would be firm, but soon it began to moan and crack, and I had to turn back. Ney said with a night as cold as this, the ice on the river would firm up, and we would try again in a few hours. We dropped down into the snow to rest and wait. I was awakened by the sound of Marshal Ney and his staff getting to their feet. Ney asked me to try crossing again and to make a signal fire when I reached the far side to guide the others. I walked across the ice with Stosh and Serge following. The ice made settling noises, but did not crack.

On the far side, we gathered wood and set to work making a fire. Ney and his staff were the first ones over. Ney thanked us and asked that we remain there, keeping the fire burning. When we could no longer see anyone on the opposite bank, we were to put all of our remaining logs on the fire and catch up to the column.

For the next few hours we continued to gather wood and help people up the bank. There were some women and children who crossed, but not as many as I had seen in the band of stragglers before the battle. The line slowed to a trickle and stopped. We built up the fire to guide anyone still out there then followed the column.

I knew the reason for crossing the river was to get away from the Russian army. Perhaps the only resistance on the northern bank would be Cossacks. As it grew light, we were all vigilant for any sign of the enemy. It didn't take long for us to spot horsemen on the horizon up ahead. "Those wouldn't be French by any chance?" Ney asked one of his officers. The officer took out his spyglass and reported they were Russians. Some stayed and watched us while the others rode off.

"Form up the column," Ney ordered. Everyone looked at each other. There were so few of us left from each regiment that it was hard to tell which regiment should join up with which. Ney took charge and began to organize the men. The size of our formation was disheartening. The number of men under arms seemed to be less than the size of a regiment.

Runners were sent back to urge the stragglers forward. It would now be critical that everyone stay close together. Then, on our right flank, the sound of horses' hooves could be heard. We turned to face the charging cavalry. They were attacking the mass of stragglers who were scattering in panic. A volley from us caused the charge to veer away and the attack was ended, but valuable time was lost in re-forming the column.

When everyone was back in order we moved ahead, taking care to keep the formation. At last we came to the road to Orsha, the next town along the route, but still many miles away. Our hearts sunk as we saw the road had already been trampled by hooves and feet.

As we moved down the road, Ney kept sending men back to encourage the stragglers to keep up. Stosh and I went on one such errand and were horrified to see how few of the stragglers were left.

We told those still walking at the end of the column that there was nothing we could do to protect them if they were not close to the soldiers. But our words had no effect on them. They were already moving as fast as they could. Others gave up and sat down in the snow, realizing their situation was hopeless.

I was surprised to find Gaston among the stragglers. I figured he had caught up with his regiment at Smolensk. Instead, here he was unarmed and wrapped in a blanket.

I wasn't afraid of him. Instead, I felt pity. The torments of the past didn't seem to matter anymore. I saw him as a fellow soldier.

Under the blanket he had on only a thin shirt. "C'mon," I said to him, "you've got to keep up."

He stopped and looked at me. "I'm not going on," he said in a quiet voice.

"You have to," I said, almost pleading. "We're the last ones in the column, the Russians are behind us."

"No," he said slowly, "I'm through. You can have my blanket." He took it from his shoulders and held it out to me as he sat down.

"Keep it. I have mine," I said, motioning to the one on the top of my pack.

"You don't have to give up, Gaston," I said, trying to reason with him. "We'll make it out, Marshal Ney knows how to..." My voice trailed off as I felt a hand on my shoulder. Stosh pulled me away, and we started back to the head of the column. I turned to see Gaston still sitting in the snow. Waiting.

Chapter 41 - The Bravest of the Brave

As we neared the front of the column, Russian soldiers began to fire from up ahead, and we ran to re-join the ranks. I looked back and saw a few of the nearest stragglers run to catch up, but there weren't many. We marched toward the enemy in formation, fired a volley and then charged. We outnumbered them and they scattered, but they soon began to take shots at us from the woods lining the road.

The officers admonished us to keep together until a cannon made its appearance up ahead. Then we were told to spread out so one shot wouldn't do as much damage. Once away from the woods, cavalry began to menace us on our right flank. We had to close ranks again to avoid being swept away by a charge.

We continued down the road in this manner, avoiding cannon fire and keeping an eye on the cavalry. None of us wanted to stop for fear of being surrounded. Ammunition was running low. When we came to a dead or wounded Russian soldier in the road, we took his cartridges.

The number of cavalry on our flank began to grow. Soon came the shout, "Form the hollow square!" Our ranks formed a square in which each side faced outward with bayonets, creating a wall of spikes no cavalryman would ride into. Men in the center of the square fired as the cavalry charged, coming as close as they dared, trying to frighten the men into abandoning their posts and causing the square to break down. With Ney in the middle shouting curses and encouragement, the square held, and the cavalry withdrew.

As the day progressed, we formed our square numerous times, fought off the attack and kept moving. By now, there were a handful of stragglers left, and we were losing soldiers in each attack.

Late in the afternoon, we came to an abandoned village where we made camp for the night. Under cover of darkness, Marshal Ney sent an officer on our one remaining horse with orders to ride to Orsha and tell Napoleon our situation so a relief column could be sent. As the officer rode off into the darkness, I said a prayer for his safekeeping, knowing our survival depended on him.

We pulled boards off the houses to make fires to thaw our frozen limbs. As with the night before, we would be gone before the fires burned out. Standing by the blaze, it seemed like an eternity ago that we had left Sergeant LaGrand and Marc to tend the fires while we made our escape. Under normal circumstances, the feeling of having abandoned them would have been overwhelming, but now, facing so much danger and seeing so many people die, my emotions were numb.

Quietly, the word was given to slip away, and our dwindling band made its way out into the forest. Away from the fire, it didn't take long for the wind and cold to freeze my hands and feet all over again. In the distance, wolves howled. It sent a shiver up my back, but I knew it wasn't the wolves we should worry about.

The sky began to turn from black to gray, and we hadn't seen any sign of the enemy. Despite our feeble condition and lack of food, our pace was fast as we attempted to travel as many miles as possible before being discovered.

Again, the first thing we saw was the enemy cavalry on the horizon and within the hour, we were fighting a running skirmish with Russian soldiers. At times, the firing became so intense, we had to stop and fight until we could force our way through. It was during one of these fights that I saw Marshal Ney had picked up a musket and joined in the firing. It gave us much needed inspiration.

As our band maneuvered away from our attackers it became less clear which direction we should be going. The overcast day hid the sun. Ney and one of his officers were having a heated discussion about which direction we were heading. I dug into my haversack and pulled out the compass I had given to Luc. I tossed it to the officer. Ney grabbed the compass, took the reading himself, and agreed we should continue in the same direction.

The Russians began to press the attack again, and Ney slipped the compass into his pocket as we returned fire. An interesting change had come over me. The day before, the attacks of the Russians had scared me. I had fired and reloaded with shaking hands, expecting to be shot at any moment. As the attacks continued, and I remained unharmed, the fear subsided, and I could calmly fire and reload.

We had to make every shot count so we were aiming at individual soldiers rather than a mass of troops as in a larger battle. I no longer felt the pangs of guilt at shooting a man as I had when Serge and I had killed the Cossack while foraging.

With the gray sky hiding the sun and the heat of battle distorting all sense of time and distance, we fought off and on through the day. Marshal Ney kept encouraging us saying it wasn't much farther and the messenger from the night before would get help. But the hours passed, and it looked like we would be spending the night out in the open without a town to provide shelter or food.

When there was a lull in the firing, the fatigue and cold began to take their effect on us. As I leaned on my gun, I heard the boom of a distant cannon. It was much too far away to be firing at us. Others heard it too. After a minute, there was another boom. It was the sound of a signal gun, not a battle.

We surged forward toward the sound. The Russians realized this was their last chance to capture or kill a French Marshal. They resumed the attack with a new fierceness.

We pressed on and felt invincible after having survived so much. Ney began shouting that we would soon be able to see our own troops. All the while he kept firing at the Russians just like the rest of us. Off in the distance, in the fading light, we could see a mass of men approaching. They were French! The Russians on our flanks began to withdraw. We ran through the deep snow. Our two groups met with embraces and laughter. Together, we marched the last three miles into Orsha.

Our arrival was greeted with cheers. Having fought through the Russian roadblock themselves, they knew we had been cut off and had given up on ever seeing Marshal Ney and his men again. Less than a thousand of us had made it through, but our survival had given hope to the army. We felt that we could do anything.

When Napoleon heard the news, he was overwhelmed and issued a proclamation calling Marshal Ney "The Bravest of the Brave."

Chapter 42 - The Berezina

That night, men willingly shared their fires and even some food with those of us who had survived with Ney. Our stories lifted their spirits so they were eager to hear them.

The weather even cooperated for the next few days. No more snow fell and the temperatures were above freezing during the daylight hours as we headed to the Berezina River. While we were glad for the warmer weather, we were counting on the Berezina to be frozen enough to cross. A few days earlier, in order to keep the army from being bogged down, Napoleon had ordered the bridge train wagons burned. Without the pontoons for making temporary bridges and the equipment needed to assemble them, we would need ice to cross the river.

As we neared the river, the temperatures dropped, snow began to fall, and the wind picked up. By nightfall, a blizzard was howling. Unable to get a fire started, Serge, Stosh, and I huddled together.

Serge had been injured in the running battle, and we could tell he was in a lot of pain, but he was unwilling to take off his coats and shirt to examine the wounds. It was a long cold night. In the morning, the snow had stopped, but the wind kept blowing. Many men were unable to get up. Some froze where they slept while others, unable to move, asked to be left behind.

A large number of women and some children were still with the column. While only soldiers had survived from the rearguard, the other corps had their own group of camp followers and stragglers. In amongst this group were men of all ages who were not soldiers. They were either civilians who were retreating with the army or teamsters whose wagons had been abandoned.

We arrived at the town of Borisov on the Berezina River the next day. Upon seeing the river, hope went out of the army. Instead of solid ice, we saw floating chunks. While the commanders huddled together discussing our next course of action, we saw Russian soldiers on the far bank.

We were ordered to withdraw from the river. A scouting party had found a suitable place to cross upstream so while one corps headed south as a diversion, the remainder of the army headed north to a town called Studenka. By evening, General Eblé and his engineers were working on making trestles for two bridges that would have to span the river for a distance of about 100 yards. We found that General Eblé had not destroyed the entire bridge train. He had kept some blacksmith forges and other equipment that was now vital to the army's survival.

Through the night, we sat and waited while the work of building the trestles went on. Early the next morning, engineers waded into the river up to their chests and worked for hours positioning the trestles on which the bridge would rest. In the meantime, we went into the town and pulled down walls and pried the siding off the houses to make planks for the roadway of the bridge.

During all of this, a handful of Russians sat watching on the far side of the river. They made no attempt to stop the work. We found out later that the main body of Russians had followed our one corps south. The diversion had worked.

The first bridge was completed in the afternoon, and our corps crossed over to defend the far side if the Russian main force arrived. Crossing the bridge was difficult as there were gaps between the planks which were not nailed down to begin with. The bridge had no railings so care was needed to keep from slipping or being bumped off into the water.

While our corps watched for the enemy, the rest of the army began to cross. Only armed soldiers were being allowed over for now. The stragglers pushed close to the bridge, but were denied access, creating a jam that slowed the progress of soldiers. Later in the afternoon, the second bridge was completed, and the artillery began rumbling across.

As we stood in formation, stamping our frozen feet and anticipating the appearance of the Russian army, there was a crash behind us followed by the screams of the crowd. Part of the first bridge had collapsed throwing people into the water. The waiting crowd surged toward the second bridge, and the soldiers guarding the entrance had to hold them back.

After a few minutes, engineers entered the water to repair the broken trestle. They worked in icy water up to their shoulders. When they came out, their clothes immediately began to freeze. I don't believe they survived the days that followed, but everyone who escaped from Russia owed their lives to those men.

In the middle of the night, I was lying near the fire when there was another crashing sound. I jumped to my feet to see that a section of the second bridge had broken. Several of the engineers had waded into the water while one of their men appeared to be looking for wood to span the gap. The engineers in the river called for him to pull up a plank and lay it over the gap so he could climb out to the trestle and hammer in a metal brace. This would have to be done while they held the legs in place. The sooner the braces were attached, the sooner they could get out of the water. He was a heavy man, and he looked at the planks doubtfully. As he hesitated, I stepped forward.

"I'll do it," I said, "I'm lighter, and it won't be so hard for them to hold the trestle up while I work on it."

We both went out to the edge of the gap, where he pulled up a plank and laid it out to the damaged trestle. All of the equipment for making the repair was still on the opposite bank. Someone laid a plank out to the trestle from the other end of the gap. I carefully balanced myself on the planks and crossed over to the other side. An officer handed me a small pouch of forged nails, and I looped the drawstring around my wrist. Then he gave me the hammer and said, "Don't drop this, whatever you do, it's the only one we have." I looked past him at the huddled masses on the shore still waiting to cross and began to doubt I could do the job. I shook as I worked my way back out to the trestle where the men in the water had propped it up with a new support. They held it in place and urged me to get to work.

I was just a few feet above the water, and I was terrified. One way or another, I was sure I would die if I fell in, if not from drowning, then from freezing to death. If I dropped the hammer, that would be a disaster too. With the eyes of the army and the stragglers on me, I began to sweat as I set to work.

I put the brace in place and, holding a heavy nail with my frozen fingers, I tentatively tapped it into one of the holes in the brace.   Someone from below shouted, "Harder!" in Dutch. Though I couldn't understand the language, the meaning was unmistakable.

I could barely make my frozen hands respond, and as I began to swing the hammer with force, the nail dropped away and splashed into the water below. I pulled another nail out of the pouch and set it in place. I found if I concentrated on the nail, instead of my hands, they worked better. With strong strokes of the hammer, I got the first nail in. My confidence grew, and I finished the job quickly. When I had pounded the last nail in place, the engineers hurried to get out of the frigid water.

I made my way back across the plank and handed the hammer back to the officer. He shook my hand and said, "Well done." Already, men were laying planks over the now secure gap. I was soon back on my side of the river. Wagons and artillery started streaming over the bridge again while I went back to my fire and collapsed in relief.

The sound of drums beating the alarm woke me with a start. The Russians had arrived. I glanced back at the bridges and could see there was still a mass of people waiting to cross, the sheer numbers crowded around the entrances made it difficult for anyone to get through. We would have to keep fighting to hold our ground until the far bank was clear.

Our ranks were made up of men from many different regiments and nationalities, pulled together to form make-shift units. Serge, Stosh and I had managed to stay together. As the Russians appeared, we gave them a volley hoping to cause disarray before they could fully deploy, but they kept coming.

We marched forward to get more distance between us and the bridges and began to exchange volleys. Throughout the morning we advanced and retreated and advanced again. We knew we had to hold the bridges at all cost. During a lull in the fight, I could hear firing on the far bank of the river. The Russian army that had been pursuing us on that side had arrived.

Off to the right, what was left of our cavalry charged the Russian positions, throwing them into disarray. We advanced to take advantage of the situation and drove the Russians back. Night was falling, and we still held the bridges.

My elation at the victory was short, however. Our ranks were thrown into turmoil during the last charge, and I couldn't find Serge or Stosh. Panic welled up in me, and I began to hurry along calling and looking for them. They were the last of my platoon. Without them I would be on my own.

Marshal Victor's men, who had been fighting on the far bank, covering the evacuation, were now crossing over to our side. We would be leaving in the morning. The fear of losing my last two friends gripped me, and I couldn't stay still. I walked through the camps looking at every man around each fire. When I thought I had searched the campfires as far as would be reasonable to go, I started to search the battlefield. It was a bright, moonlit night as I began the gruesome task of looking at the bodies in the area where our unit had fought.

Across the river, I saw a curious sight. The bridges were empty, yet thousands of stragglers could be seen just sitting on the far bank. Now was their opportunity yet they didn't move. I couldn't fathom why they would wait when the Russian army would attack in the morning.

But I couldn't spare any more thoughts for them, my own situation was desperate. I was too exhausted to continue looking for my companions. I lay down wrapped in my blanket and was soon asleep.

The sounds of movement woke me, and I could see that the column had already started off. I was almost left behind. As I rolled my blanket and gathered my gear, I heard an agonized cry go up from the far bank. The engineers had set fire to the bridges to prevent the Russians from pursuing us. The stragglers who had spent the night on the far side were trapped. They wailed and screamed as their means of escape went up in flames.

Chapter 43 - Heading Home

I turned my back on the horrifying scene at the bridges and hurried to catch up with the column. The next few days and nights were the coldest we had experienced. It was too cold to fight so the Russians left us alone.

I wasn't the only one who had been separated from my friends and regiment. When the column stopped for the night, I could hear men walking through the camps calling out "First Corps" or "Fourth Corps." They had given up looking for specific regiments because most of those had disbanded.

The army was in such a shambles that I didn't think there even was a rearguard. The city of Vilna was our next destination where it was rumored we would stay for the winter. As before, each man hoped it would be our salvation with plenty of shelter and stockpiles of food. I had my doubts that any such place existed.

During the march there, I tried to attach myself to groups of soldiers each night. Those that included some women were generally more sympathetic and allowed me to share the warmth of their fire. I kept moving during the day looking for Stosh and Serge. Some nights I was treated as an outcast and could not get near a fire even for a few minutes.

After nights like those, my body was so numb that every movement took great effort. I began to think I would not ever see home again. I felt very alone and was close to sitting down in the snow and giving up. Only the memory of Sergeant LaGrand's order to stay alive kept me going.

When I reached Vilna the scene was even worse than at Smolensk. Men were fighting with each other. Women were clutching crying children. Houses were burning. Men were being robbed right out in the open. Military discipline was gone, and there was no one to turn to for protection. I was afraid for my safety. As I ducked around a corner, I ran into someone.

I stepped back, expecting to be hit or shoved to the ground, but the man said, "Henri? Is that you?"

Looking up, I saw Stosh. We stared at each other in amazement. I spoke first, "Where were you?" I asked.

"Looking for you," was his answer.

Grabbing my elbow, he said, "C'mon, I know where the Third Corps is," and he hustled me along the street. Disorder was everywhere as we wound through the city. Eventually, we arrived at a house that had a guard posted at the door.

"This is Ney's headquarters," he explained as he led me around to the back of the house where a make-shift camp was set up and a camp fire was blazing.

"Napoleon went on ahead a few days ago so he could get back to Paris and start raising a new army. Marshal Murat is now in charge. We were supposed to stay here for winter quarters, but the supplies have been looted and nobody can control the troops."

As Stosh finished, there was a distant boom. Screams and shouts could be heard all over the city. "The Russians are here," Stosh gasped.

The sound of cannons continued as an officer ran up to Ney's headquarters and went inside. A few minutes later, Marshal Ney himself burst out of the house and announced to anyone within earshot that we were abandoning the city. Stosh grabbed his blanket and musket and we joined the crowd following Ney.

I looked around, "Where's Serge?" I asked.

Stosh looked at me, "I don't know. I didn't see him after the battle at the bridges. Something might have happened to him in the last charge."

"I looked everywhere on the battlefield for Serge and you," I said.

"Maybe we'll run into him somewhere in the column." Stosh said hopefully.

"Sure," I agreed, but we both knew that a lot of men had been left behind and would never be found.

The mob came pouring down the street, heading for the far end of the city and the road west. Ney told us to hold steady while they passed and stay together as it was up to us to protect the army. While we waited, I could hear Ney cursing about, "Murat running like a scared rabbit," and how the army was panicking over the appearance of "a few Russians who are just as cold and hungry as we are."

As we marched west, the brutal cold became our friend as it kept the Russians from pursuing. Had they made any attempt to engage us in battle, we all would have been lost. I made sure to stay close to Stosh and the companions he had joined on the way to Vilna. Some of the men had been able to get to the provisions there and were willing to share in exchange for some salt and a few pages from my book to start their fires.

After five days, we came to stand on the banks of the Nieman River. On the other side was the safety of Poland and the road home. I looked forward to seeing the Gerrards again and maybe even father. I thought about Luc's letters from Cressida in my haversack. I dreaded the moment that I would have to hand them back to her and see the pain on her face.

When the stragglers had safely crossed the bridge, Ney gave the order for his corps to follow. As I walked by, Ney called me aside. He dug into his haversack, pulled something out and handed it to me. It was the compass I had given to him during our escape from the Russians on the Smolensk road.

"I think I know the way from here," he joked as we both started across the bridge. "I've watched you these past few weeks, and I'm honored to have you in my corps. If we had a thousand men like you we'd be in St. Petersburg by now."

I blushed and mumbled, "Thank you," as I stepped off the bridge just ahead of Marshal Ney. I had been the first Frenchman in and the second to last Frenchman out of Russia.

Epilogue - A Warm Fire

A s I finished my tale, I sat looking down at the worn copy of *The History of Russia* I held in my hand. Only twenty pages were left, the rest had saved my life.

The grandchildren sat silently.

"Does it make you sad, Grandpa?" Helene finally asked.

"Yes," I said, wiping a tear from the corner of my eye, "but I would not trade the experience for anything."

"That is the necklace from Moscow!" she exclaimed looking at the shiny silver cross my wife always wore.

The children stared in amazement. Helene asked to touch it, but the boys wanted to hold the book.

"Be careful," I warned, "I'm not finished reading it yet."

They gazed in wonder as they turned the book over and over in their hands.

"Look at the time," exclaimed my wife. "Up to bed," she said as she stood to accompany the children upstairs.

I was alone with my memories, thinking of how fortunate I had been and how many good men and women had helped me along the way. When my wife re-joined me, we sat in our rockers holding hands and listening to the wind whip against the snug house.

"I love you, Henri," she smiled.

"I love you too, Cressida," I replied.

Glossary

Army Units: There are four different unit sizes mentioned in the book. They are, in order of size from largest to smallest: Corps, Division, Regiment, Company and Platoon. Henri ended up in the 3rd Corps, 11th Division, 18th Regiment, Captain Blanc's company, Sergeant LaGrand's platoon.

Haversack: Since uniforms of the period did not have pockets, a cloth sack was carried with a strap going over one shoulder. A soldier used this to carry personal items and maybe some rations. A haversack worn in this way hung near the waist so it was also more accessible than a pack. Note: Some soldiers had pockets sewn into their uniforms.

Muzzle: The open end of the barrel of a musket or cannon. This would be the opening where the ball would come out. Weapons of the day were loaded by putting the powder and shot down the muzzle rather than at the opposite end, the breech, which is how modern weapons are loaded.

Musket: The weapons of the period were flintlock muskets. These weapons were prone to misfires and could only fire one shot before they needed to be reloaded. They lacked rifling, grooves inside the barrel to make the ball spin, and therefore were inaccurate except at close range.

Regimental Coat: The uniform worn by the soldiers. Often made of wool. The color of the coat and the facings indicated the regiment to which the wearer belonged.

To The Reader

While Henri Carle is a fictional character, the timeline and events of the campaign are true. Many of the incidents described and the conditions of the march are taken from first person accounts. In this section I would like to share some background about elements of the story.

Makeup of the invading army
Only about one-third of the invading army was French, the rest was made up of troops from conquered and allied countries. Among the countries represented were Belgium, Prussia, Italy, Portugal, Switzerland, Poland and Austria. In the story, the use of the term "French Army" was meant to include the allies as well.

Russian peasants
The reaction of the peasants to the invasion varied from place to place. Some welcomed the invaders while others were more resistant. There are accounts of peasants helping the French and even warning them of pending danger from the Cossacks. But there are also stories of peasants attempting to harm the invaders. During the retreat, the soldiers feared falling into the hands of the peasants who were known to torture captured soldiers before killing them.

Gift exchange across the river during the battle of Smolensk
There is an account of French and Russian soldiers watering their horses during a lull in the battle and exchanging gifts by throwing them to each other across the water.

Typhus symptoms
Typhus is a disease spread by lice, which find an army a perfect breeding ground. Typhus is sometimes called "War Fever." There are many different symptoms including the ones experienced by Luc: giddiness, headache, a temporary recovery, and then bouts of pain in the head and limbs as well as fever and chills.

The fire of Moscow
Moscow did catch on fire soon after it was occupied by the invaders and a strong wind from a storm spread the flames through a large part of the city. While the Russians claimed the French set the fires, there is evidence that the Russians did it themselves. The governor of Moscow had vowed to burn the city and ordered the firefighting equipment to be taken away or destroyed. The French rounded up and executed "incendiaries" suspected of starting the fires.

While the Kremlin, where Napoleon had gone after entering the city, did not catch fire, the flames did come close. Those around him became concerned and persuaded him to leave, but on the way out, they became lost in the burning streets. A group of French soldiers who were looting the burning buildings gave Napoleon and his party directions to escape the flames.

The loot from Moscow
The soldiers of the army attempted to carry away as much looted treasure as possible. What couldn't be carried in wagons had to be carried by the soldiers. Almost immediately after marching out of Moscow, troops began to discard the extra weight, although some managed to get their treasures all the way home. There are numerous accounts of men wearing the women's clothing that they were taking home for wives and sweethearts for warmth in the extreme cold.

Leaving the wounded behind

When the army left Moscow, many of the available wagons were loaded down with plunder. When they passed the battlefield at Borodino, owners of the wagons were unwilling to unload their treasures to make room for the wounded there. Some were piled on top of the wagons, but if they fell off, it lightened the load so there was little incentive to stop and help them back on.

The scene repeated itself at Smolensk and again when the wagons were burned or abandoned to free up the remaining horses to pull the artillery. Without wagons, there was no way to get a wounded soldier home, especially with the harsh conditions.

Looting of stockpiled supplies

On the retreat, the first units to reach a destination would often take their fill of supplies, leaving little or nothing for those that followed.

Bashkir horsemen

There is an account of Bashkir horsemen firing arrows at the French during the retreat.

The Night March of Ney

During the retreat from Smolensk in November, 1812, Ney's Third Corps acted as rearguard and was cut off from the rest of the army when the Russian army blocked his path. After failing to break through the Russian ranks, Ney left his campfires burning and headed back toward Smolensk and then turned and crossed the Dnieper River to the northern side where he hoped there would be fewer Russians to face.

The story is told that Ney's men became lost while heading to the river and Ney broke the ice of a stream to determine the direction it flowed to help them find their way. They were able to cross the river on the ice after waiting a few hours for the ice to stiffen in the cold night air. A Polish officer was sent ahead to tell the main body that Ney was still alive and was fighting his way toward them.

When he left Smolensk, Ney had 6,000 men and about twice as many stragglers. By the time he was re-united with the main body of the army, he had 900 men.

Bridges over the Berezina River

Napoleon's engineers entered the river on one of the coldest nights of the retreat to build two bridges. After the armed soldiers crossed the bridges, General Eblé was ordered to burn them to slow the pursuing Russians. During the night, he crossed over to the eastern side to encourage the stragglers to make use of the bridges before he destroyed them. It is unknown why some did not take advantage of this opportunity and were left stranded when the bridges were burned the next morning.

Napoleon left his army behind in Russia to head home

Napoleon had heard about a failed coup attempt in Paris and knew he needed to start rebuilding his ruined army. He left on December 5th to race home to work on shoring up his now shaky empire. The army straggled out of Russia on December 14th.

Ney was the last Frenchman out of Russia

The legend is that Ney was the last Frenchman to leave Russia. By this time, the Russians had given up pursuing their enemy.

Sources

Print:

Brett-James, Antony, 1812 - *Eyewitness Accounts of Napoleon's Defeat in Russia*, Reader's Union, 1967.

Du Faur, Faber, edited and translated by Jonathan North, *The Illustrated Memoirs of Faber du Faur*, 1812, Greenhill Books, London; Stackpole Books, Pennsylvania, 2001.

Foster, John, "The Bravest of the Brave", *Boys' Life*, April, 1970, pp 34-38, 62.

Palmer, Alan, *Napoleon in Russia: The 1812 Campaign*, Simon & Schuster, 1967.

Rothenberg, Gunther Erich, *The Napoleonic Wars*, Harper Paperback, 2006.

Talty, Stephan, *Illustrious Dead: The Terrifying Story of how Typhus Killed Napoleon's Army*, Crown, 2009.

Zamoyski, Adam, *Moscow 1812: Napoleon's Fatal March*, Harper Perennial, 2005.

Internet:

"18e Régiment D'infanterie De Ligne - Wikipédia." *Wikipédia, L'encyclopédie Libre.* 23 Nov. 2010.
<http://fr.wikipedia.org/wiki/18e_régiment_d'infanterie_de_ligne>.

"Battle of Borodino, 1812." The Step Into Napoleon Bonaparte.
<http://www.napolun.com/mirror/web2.airmail.net/napoleon/Borodino_battle.htm>.

Sources

"French : Russian : Order of Battle : Borodino 1812." The Step Into Napoleon Bonaparte. <http://www.napolun.com/mirror/napoleonistyka. atspace.com/French_Russian_order_of_battle_Borodino. htm>.

"History & Culture of Russia / The Invasion of Russia." *Geographia - World Travel Destinations, Culture and History Guide.* 2005. <http://www.geographia.com/russia/rushis05.htm>.

"Napoleon - THE SYMBOLS OF EMPIRE." 2008. <http://www.napoleon.org/en/essential_napoleon/symbols/index.asp#aigle>.

Reese, Tim. "Uniforms of the French Line Infantry: 1804 - 1812." *The Napoleon Series.* Feb. 2010. <http://www.napoleon-series.org/military/organization/France/Infantry/Line/c_Reeselineinfantry.html>.

About the Author

Scott Armstrong drew on a lifetime of American Revolutionary War re-enacting, travel through Europe, and extensive reading on a wide range of topics, especially history, to bring Henri's story to life.

A history major in college, he first became interested in Napoleon's ill-fated invasion of Russia while taking a course on the French Revolution and Napoleon. Inspired by his teenage daughter, Helen, he successfully completed NaNoWriMo in 2010. His goal was to write a story that would appeal to Helen as well as to his son, Nathaniel, age 10. The result was *Russian Snows*.

Scott is the publisher of a family activities and resource guide called *Parents' Source* (www.ParentsSource.com). He grew up doing living history activities with his family. He and his wife, Sandie, met while re-enacting the siege of Savannah during the Bicentennial celebration. Later Scott and Sandie both participated in a parade in Paris on the Champs Elysées as part of a re-created French regiment during the 200th anniversary commemoration marking the end of the American Revolution.

Scott lives in southeastern Pennsylvania with his wife and two children. He can be reached at:

ScottArmstrong@RussianSnows.com

Made in United States
Troutdale, OR
03/01/2024

18106499R00111